Lily B.
on the
Brink of
Love

ELIZABETH CODY KIMMEL

Lily B.
on the
Brink of
Love

SCHOLASTIC INC.

New York Toronto London Auckland Sydney
Mexico City New Delhi Hong Kong Buenos Aires

ISBN-13: 978-0-439-92875-5
ISBN-10: 0-439-92875-3

12 11 10 9 8 7 6 5 4 3 2 1   7 8 9 10 11 12/0

Printed in the U.S.A.   40

First Scholastic printing, January 2007

Typography by Amy Ryan

For Dave Horowitz—
he writes, he draws, he drums,
he climbs . . . he rocks!

One

It's nice work, if you can get it. Not that I, future world-famous writer Lily Blennerhassett, intend to stay too long with a publication like our middle school's paper, the *Mulgrew Sentinel* (circulation: 517). But humble beginnings make great first chapters in biographies, as Future Biographers recording my life and work will attest. And frankly, I like the job description. Lily Blennerhassett, Advice Columnist.

In case you are worried, Dear Readers, that at age fourteen I cannot possibly have suffered enough to have acquired sufficient wisdom for advice dispensation, let me assure you that I have. Good spot for a little history lesson. You see, I met these people last summer at a wedding, these really cool people I now refer to only as La

Famille LeBlanc, and I kind of got sucked into their world. Like I was a bug, and they were a giant, glistening Venus flytrap. And I got kind of hung up on how sleek and trendy they were and totally bought into this so-called environmentalist work they said they did. Maybe you would have seen it coming. You seem like discerning, cautious readers. But I went in blind as a bat in a light-bulb factory, and I tried to do something really nice, generous, and biodegradable for them. And let's just say I got myself and my family into a nice big mess. You know— the kind where lawyers get called in and your parents walk around pale and silently hysterical. Suffice it to say justice was done in the end, and here I am, no worse for the wear, having learned the very important lesson that you Cannot Judge a LeBook by Its Cover. End of sermon.

Back to my new job. My best friend, Charlotte, of course, felt impelled to issue warnings.

"You can't take this job seriously enough, Lily," she said, adjusting her glasses and letting her hand linger on them so that she looked like she was posing for an author photograph for a physics textbook. This was not the way an eighth grader usually warmed up for a Wiffle ball scrimmage. I know. A Wiffle ball scrimmage probably seems a little too lame for eighth-grade gym. But Mulgrew is a "Safety First" establishment. If you want to play with heavy artillery, you do it in intramural sports after school. Hopefully by the time I'm generally acknowledged throughout the world as the nation's brightest literary star, Wiffle ball will be long obsolete and forgotten and you, Dear Readers, will require a detailed description of its plastic bat and hollow ball full of aerodynamic holes meant to enable toddlers to enjoy the motions of Major League Baseball without the cumbersome, expensive, and potentially lethal adult equipment. But at the time of this writing, it is still sadly contemporary.

Charlotte never warmed up for Wiffle ball or any other gym-related activity. Charlotte McGrath. Future Corporate Executive and Longtime Reader of *The Economist*. Close friend and associate of Lily Blennerhassett, current Advice Columnist. Charlotte peered at me intently.

"Just because we're only in middle school doesn't mean we can't have real and significant problems," she stated.

I gave her a look that was meant to remind her of *my* recent Real and Significant Problems with La Famille LeBlanc. Then I touched my toes in case the gym teacher was watching (okay, I *got close* to touching my toes. I air-touched them. My knees DEFINITELY experienced contact). Charlotte ignored me, or maybe the glare on her lenses was impairing her vision.

"You could potentially be some of these people's last, best hope," Charlotte continued.

Last? Best, of course, goes without saying, but *last*? In

the confusing maelstrom of stormy adolescence, surely Blennerhassett is the most immediately obvious Beacon of Aid Blinking in the Black of Night.

"This is going to require great compassion, objectivity, and attention to detail," Charlotte went on. She wasn't touching her toes, she wasn't even trying, and no one except me was noticing. "Not to mention discretion. Really, Lily, you cannot take your new responsibilities seriously enough."

"You're forgetting one very important thing," I told Charlotte, doing a little jogging in place. Charlotte looked genuinely baffled. She never forgot anything important.

"What?" she asked.

"Lipstick," I said firmly. "Does it fit the job description or not? If so, what shade? What make? Waterproof? Non–animal tested? Hypoallergenic? With or without sunscreen? What does Hilary Duff wear? Can I get her people to call me?"

Charlotte gave me a familiar, patronizing smile.

"No lipstick," she said firmly. "Lipstick is infantilizing."

"What? Tantalizing?" I asked.

"Infantilizing!" Charlotte shouted. I felt a tiny thrill. The word had fantastic potential! Provided I could get a definition. I did a deep knee bend. Most of one.

"What does that mean?" I asked her as I squatted

4

waiting for some kind of second wind to help me up.

Charlotte took a moment to look both superior and pleased in her corporate, pre–business major sort of way.

"To infantilize," she said, "is to make something childish. To turn a grown-up thing into a baby thing."

Now you and I are both thinking, aren't we, Dear Readers, that babies don't *wear* lipstick. The Future Corporate Executive had MISUSED a word! But oh, what a fabulous word! I jotted it down in the small spiral-bound notebook I had especially for moments like this. I know it isn't sophisticated; Palm Pilots are sophisticated. And laptops are efficiently high-tech. I'd spent months longing for a laptop before finally getting one for my birthday, and I use it at every available opportunity. But you can't bring one to gym class. On the other hand, notebooks—and I mean the kind from the olden days with actual paper and spiral bindings—are in the Stone Knives and Bearskins category. Read: primitive and uncivilized. But think quaint. And think budget. So I use a notebook. Because a journalist must record information while she is On the Go. I couldn't wait to use the word "infantilize" in my first advice column.

"Girls, form into Teams A and B," called our gym teacher, Miss Meaham. Miss Meaham looked like she'd tumbled right out the back door of a gym-teacher factory. Short and perky hair, stocky/powerful/athletic (choose your favorite adjective, Dear Readers) build, sweatpants, fists that were always clenched in little balls, and the signature element of every sports enabler—a whistle on a string.

"I'm B today," I told Charlotte, who knew that perfectly well.

"I'm A today," Charlotte responded, knowing I knew that perfectly well.

Wiffle ball does NOT build character, launch Fortune 500 companies, produce plot possibilities for novels, or render bad karma obsolete in any way, and Charlotte and I both knew it. But we would endure it because we were made of steel. We would endure it because we knew we were better than Wiffle ball. Because we were wise, because we were ambitious, because we had dignity. Because it was a required class.

We were splitting into teams, taking in who was A and who was B with the kind of desperate seriousness of purpose usually reserved for contestants on a survivor reality show. Miss Meaham assigned us to new teams every class. My evaluation of my fellow Bs was giving me the sinking feeling that while we might have a shot at a team spelling bee effort, we just weren't going to cut it as Wiffle ball champions.

I was contemplating twisting my ankle, looking wan and faint, or assuming the hands-over-abdomen International

6

Symbol for Cramps to get out of playing, when I spotted The Boy walking across the blacktop. The Boy. A vision of angelic perfection without wings, a song without words, the answer to all my hopes and dreams. Tall, lean without being angular, gorgeous without being prettified. Muscular without being gross. Hair a rich dark red you could spend a lifetime trying to replicate in a salon. He didn't walk, he loped like a panther, a rippling powerhouse who fears nothing because there is nothing on earth that can threaten him. He didn't look around, just stared straight ahead as he walked with this little smile on his face, because he was already perfect. And just when I thought he couldn't be more perfect, he paused, picked up a stray candy wrapper from the grass, and tossed it into a garbage can as he strode by. Character! He had character! I would not have been at all surprised if he had spontaneously sprouted a glittering golden halo and ascended into the Higher Realms. Dear Readers, can you contain yourselves?

He continued that smooth, loping stride until he rounded the corner of the building, heading toward the parking lot with a presidential sense of purpose. There is no scientist in the world who can convince me that the earth did not stop turning for the first moment that I laid eyes on The Boy, the moment I felt that jolt of breathless awe rivet me to the spot, the moment I felt the workings of an entire world briefly halt because what person, what object, what event, what amalgamation of time/space could compete with the glorious, the unutterable, the transcendent perfection of The Boy? I will not tell you that I heard music, because rationally I know that there was no string quartet loitering about the Wiffle ball game, but at the same time I can absolutely assure you that THERE WAS MUSIC. Spontaneous music, and light, now that you mention it, that commenced the moment when The Boy took his first step into the field of my vision. The moment when I turned full into the face of fate and caught sight of him. The moment when I became both the observer and heroine of my own story.

Unfortunately, that is also the moment I got hit in the head with the Wiffle ball.

"I'm really not well enough to do the dishes tonight," I told my mother. I tried to affect a little malaise. Excellent word, malaise. No relation to mayonnaise. Means a vague sense of ill health. Good for any occasion.

"Not well enough?" my mother cried. She could not have looked more astonished if I'd told her that the neighbor's dalmatian pup had just asked for advice in applying to medical schools.

"I was hit in the *head*, remember?" I said, clasping the dinner table with both hands in what I hoped was clearly Intense Exasperation.

 8

"By a Wiffle ball," she replied.

"Struck in the head by a line drive," I said firmly. "It is a miracle I didn't have to be hospitalized. I'm frankly surprised one of those paramedic TV shows hasn't called yet offering to buy rights for the reenactment. It was a tremendously gruesome accident."

"Did it leave a mark?" my father asked, peering at me around his newspaper.

"A mark?" I asked, affronted.

"On your head. Did it leave a mark?" he repeated.

"It left a mark ON MY SOUL!" I cried passionately.

My father resumed reading the newspaper. My mother began doing the dishes.

Lenny and Phyllis Blennerhassett. Someone really should apply for a scientific grant to study them. My father is an accountant and a devotee of aging, hairy-manned rock bands with names like the Nitty Gritty Dirt Band and Little Feat. My mother wears panty hose under her trousers (not pants, *trousers*. If necessary, *slacks*.). She is interested in learning home crafts, and she cleans obsessively.

I've reached a position in life where I can concede that a parental foundation of Acute Ordinariness can be beneficial to the development and well-being of the average American youngster. Meaning me. But oh, the agony!

My cousin Delia the Lawyer and her Silent Husband Ned were over for dinner the other night. Delia just picked at her food like she always does, and my mom made a comment about how she Never Eats and She's So Slender and Surely It Can't Be Healthy? Now, when most people say something like that to a skinny woman, they try to sound like they are scolding but really you can tell they are dishing out praise—good for you, lady, eating less than three cantaloupes a day and keeping yourself to a not-too-shabby size two. My mom, however, really meant the Surely It Can't Be Healthy part. So Delia started talking about how a girl can't be too careful, and how her own mother was, as she put it, a little broad in the beam, which my father later took me aside and explained meant she had a "can the size of Wisconsin." But this next bit is my point—Delia looked around at everyone knowingly and said, "Of course, we *all* become our mothers in the end. It can't be helped—it's a rule of nature."

This remark understandably concerned me. You might say it has haunted me ever since. (Yes, now that I think about it, go ahead and say it, Dear Readers. It has haunted me ever since.) And it was on my mind now, as I watched my mother take out the cordless DustBuster and VACUUM THE TOASTER. My jaw dropped in horror. One day would I, too, be unable to relax while knowing a modest collection of dried bread crumbs had accumulated at the base of the toaster? At the end of the table, my father rustled his paper, oblivious.

"Excuse me, please," I said, getting up.

Neither of my parents spoke up to stop me. Usually it is not so easy to get out of doing the dishes, but the toaster seemed to have overtaken my mother's consciousness like one of those alien pod people from a scary space movie. I walked out of the room discreetly, then made my way to the closet that is small enough to be snug, is large enough to accommodate me and a recently acquired large velvet pillow, and gets terrific cordless phone reception. I call it the Yakking Nook. I got comfortable, then dialed Charlotte's number, from memory and with my eyes closed. Because I could.

"Charlotte?" I asked as she picked up the phone.

"Speaking," said Charlotte. Obviously.

"My mother is *vacuuming* the toaster," I said.

"I hope she unplugged the toaster first."

"Delia says we all become our mothers in the end," I said, my voice wavering.

"Not necessarily," Charlotte said. My heart leaped.

"Really?" I asked.

"Sure," she replied. "Some of us become our fathers. But most of us become our mothers. It's not so bad. You've got a very clean house waiting in your future."

I made an angry snorting noise.

"Anyway, Char, that's not why I called. I called to talk about . . . Him."

"Who?" Charlotte asked.

"Him. With a capital H."

"You called me to talk about God?"

"No!" I yelled, frustrated.

"Well, it is widely accepted that Him with a capital H refers to—"

"Okay, okay, I mean The Boy. The Boy with a capital B!"

"Ah, yes. Him," said Charlotte. She might be a little too by-the-book sometimes, but she was my best friend. She knew exactly Who I was talking about.

"Okay, first of all, *where* did he come from?" I said, stumbling over my words impatiently. I'd been dying to talk to her about The Boy all day, and there hadn't been a chance to do so privately until now. Which hadn't stopped me from *thinking* about him.

"He appeared to come from the library," Charlotte said. "From that back door near the periodicals section that opens behind the girls' ball field. He must have—"

"Charlotte!" I interrupted. "I mean I have never seen that Boy before, and neither have you. School started over a month ago. WHERE did he come from?"

"Transferred? Just moved? I read an article about IBM spontaneously relocating three percent of their workforce this month with practically no notice. Some people had to drop everything and relocate if they wanted to keep their jobs. Maybe his parents work for IBM."

"IBM," I repeated. Those three letters had never sounded so glamorous before. I imagined The Boy's mother wearing a power suit and striding past the water cooler, Italian leather briefcase tucked under one arm. Wait a minute! I wasn't supposed to have thoughts like this! Corporate fantasies were Charlotte's territory.

"Interesting. But you're getting off the subject," I said.

"I guess I didn't get the memo," Charlotte said, cracking herself up with her own little business joke. "So what *is* the subject?"

"Charlotte," I said in my most important and meaningful voice. "Charlotte."

"Yes, Lily?"

"Charlotte," I said again. I don't know. Things just sound better in threes sometimes. Did you ever notice that, Dear Reader?

"Yes, Lily?" Charlotte repeated. She wasn't even getting impatient. Who was I kidding? She was probably leafing through *The Economist* as we talked.

"I may be in Love," I said a little breathlessly.

I could swear I heard a page freeze midturn.

"In Love?" Charlotte asked, sounding genuinely interested. "With The Boy?"

"With The Boy," I said emphatically. What a RELIEF to get that off my chest. I'd been carrying around that secret for HOURS!

"You never even got within twenty feet of him," Charlotte observed. "You didn't speak. He didn't speak."

"Are you saying you don't believe me?" I asked. "Are you saying you don't believe in love at first sight?"

"Of course I don't believe in it," Charlotte said firmly. "It's an entirely anticorporate notion."

"Well, I'm a writer," I began.

"Yes, you are," Charlotte said.

"I'm a writer," I repeated, "and I have a lifetime of training in how to detect Major Developments. When I read a novel, I know right away, in the very first moment, who will be a Significant Character and who won't. I always know who is going to end up with who, no matter how the author tries to trick me. Now I realize I can read life the same way. My life. And I know for a fact that The Boy is a Significant Character."

"Does that necessarily mean love?" Charlotte asked. "Couldn't he be significant in some other way?"

"He could be," I replied. "It's possible. That's the thing, Charlotte. We have to find out! We have to know! We have to discover!"

"Okay," Charlotte said amiably. "How are we going to do that?"

I had absolutely no idea.

DEAR LILY,

I am a seventh-grade girl here at Mulgrew. My problem that I want advice for is my mother. She is totally obsessed with me signing up for anything she calls extracurricular activities, because she says I need to have all this special stuff on my transcript to show colleges that I have (I'm not sure how to spell this) stick-to-it-iveness. Okay, here is the problem—most of the stuff she wants me to sign up for is so *not me*. For example, I still have a Tuesday afternoon free so far, and a Sunday midafternoon. And she wants me to do Chess Club and Mother/Daughter Reading Group during those times. Lily, I totally hate chess and the people in the Chess Club—sorry, guys—are kind of dorky. And I don't WANT to be in a reading group, I have too much to read for school already. And all the other stuff I have signed up for, which I won't go into 'cause then you'd figure out my real name, is totally against my personality and not stuff I care about or am good at. I am way stressed out and frustrated. What should I do?

Sincerely,
EXASPERATED EXTRACURRICULAR GIRL

DEAR EXASPERATED,

First, let's get some basic sentence structure out of the way. In the second sentence of the letter, the way you formed the sentence makes it sound like it is your mother who needs advice. Clarity is everything. That said, I would like to congratulate you for your innovative use of hyphens in sentence three.

Now, to your problem. Tell your mother she is infantilizing you, and she must stop. You can make your own decisions about joining groups and clubs. It's never too soon to think about college, but if your transcript and your application don't reflect the real you, you might end up in a college that is all wrong for your needs, followed by a career you hate, and possibly even a house and car you can't stand.

Explain to your mother that filling every afternoon with a different activity will not only cause your grades to suffer, it may also result in your developing a malaise that will negatively affect your performance in the activities that you do enjoy. Then you're headed for Generic Community College Central.

Exasperated, try THANKING your mother for her help first, then ASK HER ADVICE about something. Then, and only then, tell her the Chess Club and the Reading Group aren't going to happen. Try to make this sound like her idea. It usually works like a charm.

Yours,

LILY M. BLENNERHASSETT

I don't know how Charlotte does it, but by lunch the following day she had collected a small dossier of information about The Boy. His name was Colter Hendricks, which is by far the most perfect name I have ever heard. Colter Hendricks. With a name like that, a person could go places. Charlotte had also learned that he was in the ninth grade, had Mrs. Feeney for homeroom, that he had just moved with his mother from New Paltz because his parents had divorced, and that he was an extremely good rock climber.

"Where did you find out all this stuff?" I asked Charlotte, leaning over the lunch table toward her to thwart potential eavesdroppers. "How could you get this much info on The Boy so fast?"

"One of the first rules of basic business," Charlotte said as she opened her milk carton, "is to never reveal your methods to a client."

"Client? I'm a client?" I asked.

Charlotte beamed.

"I consider our relationship to be multifaceted in the best sense of the word," Charlotte said. "Which reminds me. I was in the student center this morning, and I found *this* on the bulletin board."

She handed me a piece of paper. I wasn't ready to stop talking about The Boy. But there were still twenty minutes left in the lunch period, and anyway, Charlotte and

I usually walked home together. There would be time to talk then, and plenty of privacy. I took the paper.

"What is it?" I asked.

"Read it."

"If I really was your client, wouldn't you read it *for* me?" I grumbled. But I looked down at the paper. For a minute I couldn't focus on it. My mind was still on The Boy, on his rock climbing and his devotion to removing litter from the face of the Good Earth. Then the words formed themselves into sentences, and I read them. And gasped.

WANTED TO HIRE

Writer seeks part-time assistant, one or two afternoons a week. Duties will include helping collect and organize historical research, light typing, and other administrative tasks. Familiarity with literature and proficiency in grammar and spelling a must. Five dollars an hour plus expenses. Call 845–555–3430.

"Charlotte!" I cried. "Did you read this?"

"Of course I read it," Charlotte replied, dabbing at her upper lip daintily with a paper napkin. "Why do you think I took it down and brought it to you?"

"A Real Writer!" I said. Charlotte nodded seriously.

"You've got to call, Lily," she said. "Get yourself an interview. This could be a big break for you. You might establish all sorts of publishing contacts with this job."

My heart thumped at the thought.

"But what about my advice column?" I asked.

"You can do both," Charlotte said. "You just have to budget your time and be disciplined."

I suddenly felt like the most disciplined person in the world. I mean, the idea was overwhelming, I admit. To be an Advice Columnist, assistant to a Real Writer, and In Love, all at the same time—that was a tall order. Was discipline enough?

"But I'm unpublished! Unproven! I mean, *you* know that I'm going to be a brilliant literary sensation, and *I* know that I'm going to be a brilliant literary sensation, but how can I expect a Real Writer to know that? Maybe she won't think I'm qualified!"

"Of course you're qualified," Charlotte said. "This writer will only have to meet you to realize that. Call, set up an appointment, and go be dazzling. I guarantee you, Lily, in under five minutes you'll have the job."

Her confidence was really magnetic. I wanted a little more of it.

"Do you really think so?" I asked. She gave me one of her widest smiles.

"I know so," she said. "I have complete faith in you, Lily."

I do love Charlotte McGrath.

Two

Charlotte had made me call that very minute, before lunch period ended, from the cell phone she'd won at Young Executives Camp last summer for Best Professional Networking Effort. I got an interview for that afternoon. It did occur to me that I would be missing my chance to walk home with Charlotte and talk about The Boy. But I had to go. I'd call Charlotte from the Yakking Nook after dinner.

The writer, who turned out to be a woman named Ellis Parson, lived just two streets away from school. I knew which house it was as soon as she gave me the address. A nice, writerly mock Tudor that had been for sale since early summer. And in case you, Dear Readers, are concerned that anyone would innocently toddle into a stranger's house, fear not. Lily Blennerhassett Knows Stranger Danger. I spoke to the secretary in the principal's office first and was assured that they knew all about the ad, and everything was on the up-and-up. I also called my mother and let her know where I was going. To say she was thrilled is putting it mildly.

I don't know if it was the prospect of gainful employment or the responsible manner of my behavior that was the cause of her excitement. What can I say? I live to please.

"Hello, I'm Lily Blennerhassett," I said, holding out my hand just like Charlotte had taught me.

"Why, Lily, how nice, you're right on time. I'm Ellis."

Then came my first handshake with a Real Writer.

"Come right on in. It's a bit of a mess, and I'm still unpacking boxes, so don't look too carefully. We'll go to my office."

Ellis Parson looked a little older than my mom, maybe late forties. She was wearing a pair of cotton batik pants and a large man's shirt. Her hair was its natural gray, cropped short to reveal a pair of silver, saucer-shaped earrings. In short, she looked just like I thought a Real Writer should. No frills, but with a definite flair nonetheless.

I followed her through the hallway, trying to glance

nonchalantly at the rooms we were passing by. It *was* a bit of a mess. I caught a glimpse of a kitchen with a few dishes on the counter, and a sitting room with magazines and newspapers piled around. I gave an inward nod of approval. Literary disorder, just as I had pictured it. This woman was for real.

Ellis Parson's office was at the back of the house, a square room with wooden floors and high ceilings. As soon as I stepped into it, I felt like I'd discovered some off-kilter, made-for-Lily Blennerhassett heaven. There were books *everywhere*. One whole wall held bookshelves from floor to ceiling, which were crammed to overflowing. But there were also piles of books on the floor, on the table next to the printer, on the windowsill. Sometimes, for variety, there was a pile of file folders or some CDs with a coffee cup perched on top like a statue. There was a ragged sandal leaning on a wastebasket, and a Barnes & Noble bag trying to unfold itself in a corner.

The wall over her desk and computer was covered with photos, posters, drawings, notecards covered in scribbles, and various, as the French say, *objets* (pronounced awb-jhay, Dear Readers). My eye was drawn to a framed black-and-white photo of a man. It was autographed. I looked closer and felt weak with disbelief. It was William Shatner—the original and incomparable Captain James T. Kirk of *Star Trek*. Ellis Parson had a signed picture of

Captain Kirk in her office. Even Charlotte would find this highly, *highly* impressive. She would probably know its current bidding value on eBay.

"My inspiration wall," Ellis said, gesturing toward the wall. "Gives me something to stare at when I can't type another sentence, which is often. Pull up a stool, Lily, and sit down."

There was, in fact, a tiny stool off to one side of her desk. I dragged it next to her own comfortable-looking chair and sat down. I said a silent prayer, something to the effect of don't-let-this-tip-over-and-me-fall- onto-the-floor-and-I-will-go-to-the-next-craft-seminar-my-mom-wants-to-attend-without-complaint. The stool creaked but it held. Local organic yarn making, here I come.

"Thanks for coming, Lily," Ellis said. "Let me tell you a little bit about me, and what I'm working on, and what I'm looking for in an assistant."

I smiled and nodded, mentally reviewing everything Charlotte had told me. Sit up straight. Make eye contact. Look like you're more interested in what she's saying than you've ever been in your life. Have at least two questions prepared. Be confident. Sell yourself. And what was the last one? Something about using the interviewer's name when talking. I thought I better get that one in immediately.

"Okay, Ellis," I said, smiling and sitting up very

straight and looking keenly interested. While I was busy looking very interested, I found myself wondering where The Boy was at this very moment. Maybe he was doing an after-school activity. Football? No, that didn't seem like him—he was a rock climber. Chess Club? No, I was certain he had a brilliant mind, but equally certain he did not consort with the high-IQ sort of doofus who frequented the academic clubs. Track and field? To keep in shape for climbing? Jogging around the playing field in shorts and a faded but form-fitting T-shirt? Muscular but—I instantly stopped myself. NO THINKING ABOUT THE BOY DURING THE INTERVIEW!

"I'm working on my third novel," Ellis said. She didn't seem to notice that my mind had temporarily wandered. She was, in fact, looking at her inspiration wall. "My second novel, actually; the first doesn't really count."

It seemed like a good time to nod vigorously, so I did.

"My last book took place during the Norman Conquest of England," Ellis said. I nodded again like I'd been there. In actuality I don't remember hearing anything about Norman conquering anybody. I hadn't seen that on CNN. Norman wasn't a very conquery name. Didn't matter. She wasn't going to ask me about it.

"Are you familiar with English medieval history and the Plantagenet kings?" Ellis asked.

Oh, no! A test already! It was entirely possible that I

 24

stared at her with a look of abject horror. But she didn't seem to notice. She just sat nicely and waited for me to say something.

"Um, you know, as a general thing, yeah. Sure. I don't know the . . . which king or anything. I mean, I saw *Braveheart*."

I know, Dear Readers. Could I have been any more ridiculously stupid? But Ellis just acted like we were having a very intelligent, equally matched conversation.

"Ah, Edward the First. Hammer of the Scots," she said.

Hammer of what? I had heard of the Hammer of Thor. Were they related? My interview was tanking! I was going down in flames.

"But I'm getting off the subject," Ellis added. "What I want to talk about is you."

Yay! I knew about me!

"Tell me why you'd like to be my assistant," she said.

"Well, I'm a writer too," I began.

Then I stopped myself. That sounded pretentious! Why was I telling a Real Writer this? I wondered what The Boy—(I cut off that thought immediately).

"I mean I'm *going* to be a writer," I corrected. "I mean, I write a lot. Stories, journals. And the school paper—I write for the school paper."

"Terrific!" said Ellis, beaming. "What do you write for the paper?"

"I'm the Advice Columnist," I said.

I can't help it. Even in the interview I got a little puffed up with pride. Come on. It *does* sound pretty cool.

"Excellent," Ellis said.

Then she waited for more.

"And books—I love to read," I said enthusiastically. Since this was true, it wasn't hard to act excited. Books are thrilling. If you don't think so, there is something wrong with you. I'm an advice columnist. I should know.

"So I'm interested in everything that has to do with books. I want to read, I want to write, I want to know more about publishing," I said. This came out sounding better than I thought it would.

"And your ad said proficiency in spelling and grammar a must—I'm a straight-A Advanced English student. I can't, you know, do long division to save my life, but I'm a totally excellent speller. I know how to do footnotes. I know how to do bibliographies. I know all of that stuff really, really well."

Too much? Was I overselling?

"Very good, Lily," Ellis said. "This is all very good. What I'm looking for is basically someone who will help me in whatever area I happen to need help in at the moment. I may suddenly need to know who the king of France was in the year 1159. I may need to have some notes typed up. Or a certain book tracked down. Or a phone call made. Or something done at the post office."

"I can do those things," I said.

Dumb. That was a dumb to say.

"I like to think I'm easy to work with," Ellis went on thoughtfully. "I can be distracted. I can be persnickety. But I think I'm relatively uncomplicated."

I made a note to myself to look up "persnickety" as soon as I got home. It sounded sinus related.

"As the ad said, I'm looking for someone for one or two afternoons a week. At least to start with. And I think the job has a great deal to offer someone like you, Lily. Hard work traded for experience. Jobs in publishing are hard to come by. This is an in for someone. A head start."

I was doing the nodding thing again. I should have let Charlotte spend more time coaching me. Then Ellis stood up all of a sudden. So I stood up too. Lily see, Lily do.

"Well, Lily, I've certainly enjoyed meeting you," Ellis said.

"Oh, so have I!" I responded. Which of course sounded like I had enjoyed meeting *myself*. Which was, of course, *stupid*.

"I've interviewed several students already, and I have a few more I've committed to seeing," she said. "But I have to say I have a good feeling about you."

Fortunately I stopped myself from saying "Oh, me, too."

"I have your address and phone number, so I'll be in touch, Lily," she finished.

"Thanks, Ellis," I said. Tell Charlotte, Dear Readers. I used her name to talk to her. I did something right.

I really didn't want to leave that office piled with books. I wanted to stay there, breathing in all that writerliness. I wanted to melt into a corner and watch Ellis sit down and actually write, actually type Real Sentences that were going to be in a Real Book and published by a Real Publisher. I wanted to play a part, however humble, in the Creation of Literature. Ellis Parson just had to offer me the job. She just had to.

And until then, I had a job of my own. After all, I was still Lily Blennerhassett, Advice Columnist.

DEAR LILY,

My boyfriend just gave me a sweater for my birthday. He is very particular about what I wear, and I love that he took the time to buy me a present. I want him to know how much I appreciate that. Unfortunately, the sweater is a nightmare. The colors are all wrong for me (yellow and green!) and the neckline is too high and the sleeves itch horribly. I totally cannot wear this sweater. It makes me look like a jockey for the Kentucky Derby.

Lily, now my boyfriend has tickets to an outdoor concert next month, and he wants me to wear the sweater so I don't catch cold. I don't want him to get mad at me, plus I really want to go to this concert. But I cannot wear the sweater! What do I do?

                    Sincerely,
                    FEARFUL OF FASHION FAUX PAS

DEAR FEARFUL,

I have to be honest with you—this guy sounds a mite persnickety. You know, a little hard to please in a fussy, detail-oriented kind of way. But who am I to stand in the way of Love? So here's what you do.

Obviously, you can't wear the sweater because from what you've told me you will look like sadly haggy in it. But I think we can assume your boyfriend might not be able to understand that he has vile taste in girls' clothing. So you are going to have to make him believe that, in spite of the fact that you JUST ADORE the sweater, he's going to have to exchange it. Why? Any number of reasons. Too tight in the shoulders, for example. Does your boyfriend play a sport? Tell him you're afraid if you raise your arms to cheer, the sweater will rip. Or tell him the weave is giving you a rash under the chin. Doesn't hang right in the back. Whatever reason you give, make sure you sound devastated. Then make sure you GO TO THE STORE WITH HIM to exchange the sweater for something better. If possible, make it seem like the sweater you do want was his idea. Works like a charm.

Yours,

LILY M. BLENNERHASSETT

My father was on the phone for, I swear, *hours* that night after dinner. He completely did not care that I urgently needed to call Charlotte. Why don't I have my own phone line? Why is the Blennerhassett home a NON–CELL PHONE ZONE? Not all progress is bad! Why do Lenny and Phyllis categorically refuse to step into the twenty-first century? We have no microwave oven! We have no DVD player! No TiVo! No Caller ID! No remote garage-door opener! (All right, in fairness, we have no garage either.) But excuse me, I am doing my best to advance intellectually, socially, and spiritually, and it is a LITTLE CHALLENGING to undertake this work in such primitive circumstances.

Anyway, this gives you an explanation for why I was sitting upstairs in my room staring out of my window, and why I had been in that position for the better part of a half hour. From my trusty heating vent, I could hear the sound of Dad's voice still yakkety-yakking on the phone.

My mother had run out to Stop & Shop to load up on a few new bottles of Mr. Clean. If we'd had a dog, he might have been lying near me, his head on my knee, his eyes liquid and large as he sensed a feeling of unrest in his beloved Lily. But we don't have a dog, either. Not because they are unnecessarily modern, but because they shed, and because my father has some kind of allergies.

So I was sitting there, all by myself, staring out the window, when all of the sudden The Boy rode past my house on his bike. PAST MY HOUSE! It all happened so fast, I barely knew what to do. So I did the only thing I could do—I wrote down the date and time of The Boy Sighting, and made a notation of what he was wearing. Don't sneer. These things are potentially Very Important. One day it may suit me very well indeed to know that The Boy likes a nice slate-gray fleece on a chilly day. And at some time I may have the opportunity to gently chastise The Boy for not wearing a helmet. Though if I had dark-red, glossy straight hair that fell just over my eyebrows in a casual but devastatingly gorgeous fashion, I might think twice before squeezing my head into a helmet too.

I had grabbed a brand-new notebook to jot down The Boy details. It was a nice, sewn-binding marble notebook with a cerulean blue cover ("cerulean" sounds much dreamier than saying sky blue, don't you think?). I picked up one of my nice, thin Sharpies (only a Sharpie will do when you need to write something of indelible importance) and wrote *the boy pages* in bitty letters, followed by larger letters that spelled COPYRIGHTED MATERIAL—KEEP OUT! VIOLATORS WILL BE PROSECUTED TO THE FULL EXTENT OF THE LAW.

Look, I'm not a doofus. I know keeping a notebook about the One You Love from Afar could, under certain circumstances, be a little Fifth Grade. But I am no ordinary citizen, remember. I am a writer. A writer who has experienced transcendental awareness that a Significant Character has sauntered into the plot of her life. If possible, these kinds of major life developments must absolutely be recorded, contemporaneously (learned that one last week, look it up!).

I am Lily Blennerhassett. I've Got Plot.

Three

♡ LILY'S FANTASY INTERLUDE NUMBER ONE ♡

Lily is hiking the Appalachian Trail. She climbs the steep mountain path effortlessly, her forty-pound backpack no match for her rippling leg muscles. She senses motion ahead and pauses, brushing a perfect corkscrew-curled lock of hair from her tanned but glowingly moisturized and SPF 30-protected face. She listens keenly, her bright cinnamon eyes narrowing in concentration. Someone is in trouble. Lily strides forward, rounding a bend in the path. Ahead, in the grass, a giant black bear looms over a crouching figure on the ground. It is The Boy. He is frozen, rooted to the ground in terror, but he sees Lily, and his eyes silently plead with hers.

Lily has attended a six-week intensive course in bear safety, and she knows exactly what to do. She shouts and

*stamps loudly, and the bear rears back, startled. She unclips
her antibear pepper spray from her utility belt and starts
shouting and waving fearlessly at the massive animal. The
bear hesitates, then, clearly intimidated by Lily's fortitude,
drops to all four paws and lumbers quickly away.*

*Lily goes over to The Boy and helps him to his feet. His
mouth is open in astonishment. He looks off in the direction
of the fleeing bear, then looks back at Lily. His face is taut
with awe and gratitude.*

"Who are you?" The Boy whispers.

"I am Lily Blennerhassett."

*"Lily Blennerhassett," The Boy repeats. "You saved my
life."*

"It was nothing, really," Lily says modestly.

"How will I ever repay you?" The Boy asks.

"You don't need to repay me," Lily says.

"What about dinner and a movie?" asks the Boy.

Lily's answer is in her smile. The Boy takes her hand. . . .

I was sitting at my very own desk in the basement office
of the *Mulgrew Sentinel,* conveniently located one flight
below the school cafeteria (there is nothing like the smell
of a Sloppy Joe on a bun to clear up writer's block). You
have to be intellectually oriented in some way to understand the significance, the Moving Emotional
Transcendence, of being given your own desk in a space

dedicated to journalistic excellence. Even if it is only middle school journalistic excellence.

I named my desk the Lily Pad. My friend Bonnie, who has always been More Than a Little Arty, drew a Lily Pad on some poster board and lettered the words out beneath it beautifully. I had to stop her from sketching in a frog, which I felt would have made the whole thing too frivolous. I hung it over my desk. Anyway, this inspired me to name my advice column Notes from the Lily Pad. It's okay for you to think that's clever. Between you and me, sometimes I amaze even myself.

In the interests of Full Disclosure, Dear Readers, I should tell you that before lunch I spotted The Boy near the computer center and commenced surveillance while partially obscured by a water fountain. I recorded his activities in The Boy Pages. I observed him shoving a hardcover textbook into his backpack, then followed him to his locker. It's in the red, slightly dented section next to the student activities bulletin board, fourth locker from the left if you are facing Mrs. McSweeney's homeroom. He opened his combination lock on the second try. He placed his backpack in the foot of the locker, retrieved a crimson fleece from the hook, and took a brown paper bag from the top shelf. Closing his locker, he reached into the paper bag and extracted a sandwich, possibly roast beef or ham, though I cannot completely rule out smoked turkey breast, on white bread. If he had a beverage, it remained in the bag. He could have intended to get a soda from the vending machine. Or perhaps he meant to eat the sandwich, then have a nice drink at the water fountain. Conversely, his intention may have been to swing by the cafeteria for a complimentary chocolate milk. Or orange juice. No chips or pretzels seen. When he picked up his pace and went down the staircase by the gym, I elected to cease my surveillance. I had enough information for the time being. I needed to collect myself and get on with my day.

Thus I retreated to the safe haven of the Lily Pad. I sat staring at my desk with a sense of purpose, which was harder than it sounded, because there were currently zero (0) letters in my in-box. Life seemed to be stopping me at every important juncture. I was here, poised and ready to direct the lives of my confused, distracted, or overstimulated peers, but there were no letters to respond to. I was prepared to throw myself, body and soul, into the literary career of Ellis Parson, sparing no effort, no matter how bone crunching the cost, to perform the job of assistant in a fashion so sublimely excellent that perhaps I myself might be the subject of her next book. But I couldn't, because after one week she still hadn't called and offered me the job. And I was poised on the Brink of Love, bold and graceful as a dancer, waiting for the wings of rapture to bear me hence . . . but I was stuck on the ground, because I hadn't dared to so much as make The Boy aware of my existence, except in Fantasy Land.

The door to the *Sentinel* office opened. I heard the tell-tale jangle of little bells, so I knew it was Bonnie before she got so much as one henna-dyed toe in the door. Bonnie wears tiny bells around her ankles all year round (except in the dead of winter, when she wears some kind of authentic-looking mukluks). Bonnie has a style so unique it currently has no name. (My mother once said Bonnie cultivated the hippie look, and my father countered that she emulated Stevie Nicks. Who among you, Dear Readers, even knows who this guy is?) Bonnie wears long, flowing Indian skirts and peasant blouses, thumb rings and chokers. Feather earrings. And she wears this soft, kind of calming perfume—it smells like the inside of a shop that sells Buddha statues and cone incense and Tibetan prayer bowls.

Bonnie walked into the office holding a small sketch pad in one hand and a Last Supper lunchbox in the other. She came toward me, her straight, silky hair forming a curtain around her face, à la Avril Lavigne. The soothing smell of her enlightening perfume wafted delicately around me. Her peasant blouse poofed. Sometimes I am surprised when I realize Bonnie is *not* leading a yak on a rope behind her.

"Hey, bro," she said to me, pausing by the Lily Pad.

That is another function of Bonnie's style. She calls everyone, regardless of their gender or familial relation or lack thereof to herself, "bro." Sometimes "dude" for a little variation. Occasionally "man." You get used to it.

"Hi, Bonnie," I replied. I didn't always understand Bonnie, but I liked her. I had liked her since the third grade, when she traded me her Hostess cupcake for my organic vanilla yogurt cup. When I get to wondering how I ended up with a mother who feeds me organic yogurt, sometimes I remember to also wonder how Bonnie got a mother who feeds her snack cakes. Perhaps there was some kind of food-agenda-switched-at-birth episode in our families. I don't currently have time to investigate this seriously.

"Saw the new edition of the *Sentinel*," Bonnie said, sitting on the corner of the Lily Pad. A muffled jingle issued from her right foot as she got comfortable. "Looks good. Nice going on the Fashion Faux Pas Girl. Wise words, old soul."

Being called an old soul by Bonnie was like being called buff by Madonna. It just didn't get much better than that.

"Thanks, Bon," I said. "That's really nice of you. I saw the issue this morning, too, and I have to say your sketch of the cafeteria at dawn was really something."

Bonnie nodded. This was something I was trying to

work up to—nodding when someone complimented my work. I wasn't able to do it yet, but Bonnie always pulled it off.

"I like to play around with perspective," she said. "You know, catching spaces in ways that people don't usually see them. The cafeteria at dawn is so quiet and illuminated. It was like a cathedral, you know what I'm saying?"

"I completely saw that," I said. "The tables looked like pews."

Bonnie peered at me intensely.

"Exactly, bro. Right on," she said.

Then we ran out of conversation, as Bonnie and I occasionally have the tendency to do. These silences never seemed to bother Bonnie. Her gaze drifted into the distance and her eyes got all soft and unfocused looking. At moments like this, she was a dead ringer for a pale-featured female version of Keanu Reeves. Then suddenly she gave a little shudder, and her eyes focused.

"Whoa, sorry to go OOBE on you," Bonnie said. Pronounced *oobie*. I was used to Bonnie's frequent references to Out Of Body Experiences. To me they were now as normal as my own frequent trips to the girls' room.

"No problem," I said. "I don't have much to do. I came down here to work on my column, but I have, like, no work that's come in."

"Oh, yeah," Bonnie said, opening her sketchbook. I

felt a brief surge of pride as I thought she wanted to draw me at my desk. I casually arranged myself in a cerebral pose, fingers to chin, eyes distant and deep in thought. But instead of starting to draw me, Bonnie pulled out some envelopes and papers that she had tucked into the pad. Embarassing.

"Thanks for reminding me," Bonnie said. "Saw Ms. Innis outside the faculty lounge. She asked me to drop over the *Sentinel*'s mail."

Ms. Innis was the paper's faculty adviser. She was kind of a cow, and a control freak to boot. That's off the record, Dear Readers.

I took the mail.

"Thanks," I said. "I'll put them in the right in-boxes."

"You're a pal, bro," Bonnie said, rising to her feet with a jangle. "Gotta split."

"Catch you later," I said.

"Later, man," Bonnie called over her shoulder as she chinked and dinged out the door.

Alone again. The curse and blessing of the writer. I leafed through the mail and felt a surge of excitement when I saw one of the envelopes addressed to the Lily Pad. Work! I started to open it but noticed a sheet of paper underneath it, with my name written on top. It was a phone message from the main school office, asking me to call Ellis Parson when I got a chance.

We aren't supposed to use the *Sentinel* phone for out-side calls, but this *was* industry related, after all. Trying to re-create Bonnie's flower-child artistic confidence, I took a few deep breaths and flipped my hair out of my face before dialing Ellis's number. To my dismay, there was a tremble clearly audible in my voice, and the palms of my hands were sweaty, which grossed even me out.

But it didn't matter. Two minutes of pleasant chatter later, I had myself a job.

Lily Blennerhassett. Assistant to the Author.

"I *am* pleased. Of *course* I'm pleased," my mother was saying from her standby position at the sink. She was cleaning the insides of the lids of all our condiment bottles. Dad really hated it when there was a surplus of dried ketchup on top of the Heinz jar. "It's a job, and you sought it out and got it yourself! Why would I be anything but pleased?"

"Mom, you might as well be wearing a neon sign over your head that says I'M WORRIED ABOUT SOMETHING," I said.

"Lily, don't be ridiculous," my mother replied.

Five; four; three; two; one—

"Although there is something I've been meaning to talk to you about," she continued.

Liftoff!

"What?" I said. And I want you to believe, Dear

Readers, I NEED you to believe that I said that word without ANY tone WHATSOEVER. There was NO tone. The word was TONELESS. Tone free. Anti-tone. A non-tone-zone.

"Now don't get irritated with me before I've even said anything," my mother said, drying and buffing the ketchup lid until it gleamed like the Star of Bombay.

"I'm not irritated!" I said.

"You had kind of a tone," she replied.

TELL HER THERE WAS NO TONE! Forget it. I'll do it.

"There was no tone, Mom," I said. "Honest. Go ahead."

My mother contemplated the lid to the Gulden's mustard. It was kind of encrusted. I could see it all the way from where I was sitting, at the kitchen table.

"Well," she began carefully, "as I said, Lily, I'm very pleased about your job. I was pleased when I first heard you were going to respond to the advertisement. I thought it was very ambitious of you, particularly since you already have a job with the *Sentinel*. And naturally, I'm even more pleased to hear you've been offered the job."

Someone is giving her a dollar, I mused, for every time she uses the word "pleased" in a sentence.

"Your father and I both think it's terrific, Lily. We couldn't be more pleased."

Cha-ching. Seven dollars.

"I just want to make sure that you—oh, how do I put this delicately. . . ."

Uh-oh. Delicately is never good.

"Just spit it out, Mom," I said. Geez, now she was starting to make ME nervous.

"It's just that you're so passionate about writing and about books, Lily," she said.

Duh. And?

"Which is one of the things I love best about you. I'm more pleased than you know to have a literary daughter."

Cha-ching. Eight.

"I just want to make sure you remember, honey, that this writer, this Ellis Parson, is a *person.*"

Wait, let me get CNN on the phone for this major news flash.

"Mom, of course she's a person."

"I just mean that . . . I'm sure she's a wonderful . . . I know, actually, that she's a wonderful writer. Just don't make her into something she's not, Lily. That's all. She's just a person who happens to be a writer, and she's probably flawed like anyone else."

Ah, yes. My Universal Translator was now completely operational, and I understood what my mother was trying to get at. I was, possibly, a little prone to idolizing people last summer. So much so that it never occurred to me that my heroes La Famille LeBlanc might actually be rat finks. Which, as it turns out, they were. And now my mother was worried I was going to idolize Ellis Parson. But why she would think such a thing I cannot imagine.

"What are you wearing, by the way? I've never seen you in those clothes, Lily."

I had, in fact, made a brief visit to the Jumble Trunk Thrift Shop on my way home from school. I had indeed acquired the makings of several new outfits, at the bargain price of three dollars per plastic bag full of clothes. I did happen, at the moment, to be wearing a newly acquired large denim shirt over faded Balinese dancing pants, and a pair of plate-shaped, imitation-silver earrings dangled and jingled deftly from my ears. Okay, maybe it was a slight departure for me. But anyone could see it was an outfit of a serious-minded scholar, a reader, an intellectual. A Real Writer.

I glanced down at my outfit and felt an inner flush of pleasure. I then looked innocently at my mother. "What?" I asked.

"You just don't look like yourself," she said.

"How can you possibly know that? Maybe this is the first day in my entire life that I HAVE looked like myself."

My mother gave a little sigh and began buffing the mustard lid she had in her hand.

"Maybe so, Lily. I just think a person's true self comes from what they feel within, not from what they see outside."

How sharper than a serpent's tooth than to have a mother who HAS A POINT.

"Okay, okay," I said hastily. "I get it, Mom. You probably think I'm dressed this way because of Ellis. Maybe I did in some vague way get the idea from her, but these clothes just happen to be *extremely comfortable.* This outfit expresses my true self because of its *lack of constriction.* This doesn't mean I'm going to start worshipping Ellis or something and then watch her turn out to be some bloodsucking ogress."

"Well," my mother said, screwing the buffed and gleaming lid back onto the mustard, "I don't know that I'd put it quite that way. But you do have the tendency to be just a little quixotic sometimes, and I just want to help open your eyes a little."

Quick-zotick? I usually don't like to ask anyone but Charlotte (and Merriam-Webster) what a word means, but this one sounded too tantalizing to pass up. And besides, it was only my mother.

"What's quick-zotick?" I asked.

"Oh, you know, honey," she said. "Quixotic means sort of prone to foolishly idealizing things. It's from the character Don Quixote from that old Spanish book.

You know, one of the classics."

"Ah. Well don't worry. I was quick-zotick *last* summer. This is the new me. I'm going with something more, well, *exotic* this year." I said, thinking momentarily of The Boy.

"Well, you seem to understand what I'm saying," she said, wrenching the lid off a jar of mango chutney. "And that's all that really matters."

She doesn't get my little puns. Never has.

"I do understand, Mom. Don't worry. I'll be fine. And what did you mean when you said you actually know Ellis Parson is a good writer?" Abrupt subject change, I know, but I was curious for the answer.

"Oh, I thought her name sounded familiar when you first told me about her, and it turns out I've read her novel about the Norman Conquest," she said. "It was really good. I think this is very exciting for you, Lily. Ellis Parson is very talented. She's the real thing."

"You read her book?" I asked, excitedly. "I mean, without knowing I was going to be working for her or anything, you just happened to have read her book?"

My mother nodded.

"It was good," she repeated. "Wonderful historical detail. I envy you, Lily, really I do. You're going to have fun at this job. I'm really, really pleased."

Cha-ching.

46

DEAR LILY,

My best friend says if I do not make the cheer-leading team, I might as well not even exist at Mulgrew Middle School. She says if I want to hang out with the best crowd, cheerleading is a requirement. Between you and me, I think cheer-leading is kind of stupid and not all that flattering to the female image. But I do want to exist at school. I do want to hang out with the best crowd. Is my friend right? Write back fast, because try-outs are next week.

> Yours,
>
> SEEKING SOCIAL SAVVY

DEAR SEEKING,

Your friend is a quixotic termagant. I'm not inventing this—look it up in the dictionary if you have time between sucking up to "popular" kids. Sorry to be so harsh, Seeking, but you need to have some sense knocked into you FAST.

Read my lips (because I'm moving them while I write): The BEST crowd is the crowd that makes you the happiest, the one where you fit in without pretending to be somebody else. Is it possible you can have reached middle school without learning this?

Do what makes you happy with the people who make you happy. It's that simple, Seeking. Otherwise you're going to be faking it for the rest of your life, and I can guarantee you, you might end up in the popular crowd, but they won't like you, and you won't like yourself either.

Now go read something!

Sternly,

LILY M. BLENNERHASSETT

"What's with the copy of *Rock & Ice* magazine?" asked Charlotte as we stood in line anticipating a piping-hot, hearty meat-and-gravy entree. We ended up getting a lukewarm, lackluster stack of nuggets with liquid blanket instead.

"What copy of *Rock & Ice*?" I said loudly.

Charlotte gave me a long look over the rims of her new glasses. You know, everything they say about glasses (that I'm aware of) is true. Charlotte has looked extremely smart since the day she was born. But now, with those glasses on, she looked like some kind of rocket engineer, the kind who could perform a little emergency brain surgery on the side if absolutely necessary.

"The one faceup on your tray. The same one that was faceup on your desk during study hall, and faceup on the floor outside your locker before that. The same one, if I'm

48

not mistaken, that has been sticking out of your book bag all morning—at least the top two inches of it, where it says *Rock & Ice* in red letters."

"Oh, that one," I said. Then I reached for a chocolate pudding cup with one hand while signaling with the International Lily/Charlotte Gesture for "come sit down and don't speak of it out loud until we have some privacy."

Charlotte, lord love her, complied.

"Well?" she said when we were safely at a small table far away from the others.

"The magazine is for research," I said.

"For Ellis?" Charlotte asked, raising her eyebrows. "I thought you didn't start until today."

"Research on The Boy. You said he's supposedly an expert rock climber."

Charlotte looked simultaneously alarmed and irritated.

"Lily, don't you read your own column? That letter you showed me about the cheerleader girl was excellent, and true, and you know it. But it's supposed to be okay for you to pretend to be into rock climbing to get The Boy's attention?"

"I'm not going to pretend I'm into rock climbing!" I said, bristling.

"Then what?" Charlotte pressed.

"I'm going to educate myself about rock climbing and see how interesting I might find it," I said. "And in the process, if I should happen to run into The Boy and we should happen to begin talking, I can ask intelligent questions about his climbing experience. This will show him that I am polite, well educated, and genuinely interested in his thoughts and experiences. This will significantly increase the chances that he will Like Me."

"Hmmmmmm," Charlotte said. The crease that formed between her eyebrows when she was thinking was particularly deep at the moment.

"What?" I asked.

Charlotte held up one finger. She's got the kind of personal energy that, when she holds up one finger, you automatically wait without getting mad.

"Okay," she said after a moment. "I just wanted to think it through very thoroughly and make sure it had complete integrity. I understand now that you've explained it, and I think it's a good idea."

"Great, then. I'm pleased," I said.

Dear Readers, TELL ME I did not just say that I was "pleased" like my mother. If I begin to vacuum a toaster, have me TAKEN AWAY!

"I'm happy you think it's a good idea, I mean," I corrected.

When Charlotte placed her seal of approval on something, it was like having it endorsed by the Nobel Prize committee. You knew it was airtight.

"Hey, bro."

I hadn't heard Bonnie's jingling over the cafeteria noise. I smiled at her and gestured toward a seat.

"Thanks, man," Bonnie said. "Hey, Charlotte."

Charlotte was the only person Bonnie did not address by a masculine nickname. Charlotte alone retained her full, womanly identity in Bonnie's presence. I am not certain why.

"Hi, Bonnie," said Charlotte. "Cool ring."

"Thanks," Bonnie said, holding up her hand and examining it. "Came from a Tibetan dairy farm."

I wanted to ask if Bonnie had obtained the ring in person, and if she'd done any milking herself while in Tibet. Yak milking, possibly. But Bonnie's gaze had fallen onto my magazine.

"*Rock & Ice*. Excellent," Bonnie said. She looked at me. "Yours?"

I nodded, glowing in spite of myself at the implied endorsement. Between me and Charlotte, apparently I looked the more likely candidate to have a copy of *Rock & Ice* magazine. This was progress.

"Radical! Do you climb?" Bonnie asked.

Charlotte began mixing whipped cream into her pudding with an amused expression on her face.

"I'm interested in it," I said. I was going to leave it at that, but something in Bonnie's open, serene expression made me want to explain. I was dying to talk about The Boy. Bonnie might provide valuable new insights. And besides, Bonnie had once told me that groups of friends and family members tend to reincarnate with one another lifetime after lifetime. If this was true, I had probably already confided to both Bonnie and Charlotte in past lifetimes about past incarnations of The Boy. Bonnie probably had centuries of experience she was just waiting to share.

"To be honest, there's this new guy at school I'm hoping to meet, and I heard he's really into climbing."

"Must be Colter Hendricks," Bonnie said.

It was only through sheer force of will and the cooperation of gravity that a stream of pudding did not at that moment come spurting out of my mouth. How could she have known that straight off? This HAD to be a past life episode continuation!

"Charlotte told you?" I spluttered.

Charlotte looked outraged but did not stoop to speaking while her mouth was full.

"No way, man," Bonnie said. "Just using my intuition."

"Do you *know* him?" I said. (Okay, I shouted. Or maybe it was more of an exclamation. Either way, it was loud. Bonnie didn't seem to mind.)

"My brother Jake does, so I've seen him around." Bonnie replied. "Jake's real into climbing, and this guy Colter has won, like, competitions and stuff. They've done some of the same routes up at the Gunks. Which means Colter must do trad climbs, too, not just sport, 'cause there's no bolts in the Gunks."

"Okay, wait," I said, producing my notebook. I had been HONEST, after all, in proclaiming why I was interested in climbing. And Bonnie clearly had a multilife understanding of these issues as they related to The Boy. So there was no shame now, was there, if I took a few notes for later accuracy? Charlotte was watching us both with detached interest.

"Okay, define gunk, trad, and sport," I said, my pen ready. Bonnie was nodding like a horse that sees someone approaching with a handful of sugar cubes.

"Yeah. Well, it's *the* Gunks first, bro. The Gunks. It's this wicked ridge of cliff face up in New Paltz. Best climbing in the northeast—climbers come from, like, all over to try it."

Gunks, I wrote.

"*The* Gunks," Bonnie corrected. "It's short for the Shawangunks."

When Bonnie's spirit was not separated from her body and traveling the astral world, she was really quite on top of things.

"And trad and sport are two different ways to climb, and you know how people get, man. Trad is short for traditional. The trad climbers think sport climbers are wussy and destructive, because they use tools to drill into the rock and place permanent bolts there to hook into. The sport climbers think the trad climbers are just elitist loud-mouths. But there's no rap bolting in the Gunks—you can only use removable gear. Sink your pro and clean it as you go. Colter's probably a trad climber when he's not competing. Could do some bouldering, maybe."

Apparently this sport came with an entire language of its own, with new words used in new ways. I LIKED this sport!

"Dude, what are you doing, taking notes?" Bonnie asked. She had only vegetables on her tray. Trying to maintain a highly nutritious meal plan at Mulgrew was like trying to keep a pair of Stuart Weitzman boots shiny while walking through a horse barn. But Bonnie did pretty well.

"Yes, exactly, I'm taking notes," I said. Lily Blenner-hassett, Completely Honest Person.

"Excellent," Bonnie replied. She picked up a green bean with her fingers and contemplated it. I had the feeling she could see The Universe inside it.

"Are you ready for this afternoon?" Charlotte asked, scraping the last of her pudding from the cup. Charlotte was a master of the Abrupt Subject Change.

"I think so," I said. My stomach fluttered a little, but it might just have been the lunch.

"Is that what you're going to wear?"

"Yes. What? Why?" I glanced down at myself. I was wearing the Balinese dancing pants again and a plain white Gap T-shirt. Simple. Scholarly. Understated. Dangerous around tomato sauce.

Charlotte shrugged. I knew Charlotte well enough to know some advice was on its way.

"What you wear is a visual indication of how you see yourself in relation to your professional abilities," Charlotte said.

"This is publishing, Charlotte, not international business law. This outfit shows that I prioritize creativity over fashion."

Bonnie interrupted her bean contemplation to look over at Charlotte.

"Whoa," Bonnie said. "Are we not talking about rock climbing anymore?"

"Lily got an afternoon job as an assistant to a writer," Charlotte said, not without a touch of pride. In spite of all my weird, noncorporate literary aspirations, Charlotte was still determined to mold me in her image. To whatever extent that was possible.

"Excellent!" Bonnie cried.

"Well, I see myself as bringing brain and passion to Ellis," I said, sitting up straight and lengthening my neck à la Gwyneth Paltrow. "I'm about substance, not form. Intellect, not image."

"I still think there's something missing," Charlotte insisted. "Something a little sophisticated. I get that writers are supposed to look casual, but that doesn't mean you should completely lack polish. Especially not on your first day."

What was I supposed to do? I was due at Ellis's house at three thirty, directly after the last bell. There wasn't exactly time for a makeover.

"Try this," Bonnie said. She put her bean down and unfastened the necklace that she was wearing—an oval-shaped piece of silver framing a shimmering, fragmented piece of glass. Around the glass were etched little words. I put it on.

"Hey," Charlotte said. "Now that's something."

"Righteous," Bonnie proclaimed.

I stared down at myself. I could see part of the necklace just past my chin, but I couldn't get any real idea of the effect.

"It's a piece of glass from a two-thousand-year-old archeological site in Israel," Bonnie explained. "The writing is from Dante's *Inferno*."

"Perfect," Charlotte said. "Sophisticated, literary, and topical. Nice, Bonnie."

"Are you sure?" I said, poking nervously at the necklace. "Bonnie, what if I lose it?"

"You won't lose it, man," Bonnie said, turning her attention back to her bean. "Not unless you're meant to. Wheel of fortune, you know what I'm saying?"

I had, in fact, no idea at all what she was saying, but the necklace seemed awesome. I nodded.

"Now you're ready," said Charlotte.

"Am I?" I asked. I was starting to feel nervous again.

"You're going to rock, dude," said Bonnie.

Then she popped the bean into her mouth.

Four

At precisely three thirty (Charlotte had emphasized REPEATEDLY the importance of absolute and utter punctuality), I knocked on Ellis Parson's door. I was ready. I knew exactly what degree of smile to have. I had three pleasantries prepared, two serious references to current literary works, and four possible places to put my hands so I did not look like a doofus. I was ready to jump into work immediately, and I was equally ready for the possibility that Ellis might like to indulge in a little getting-to-know-you time. I was prepared to type, to read, to index, to reference. In short, I was prepared for any possible eventuality in the probable scheme of The Universe.

Except for the one where The Boy answered the door.

In the time it took my jaw to drop so that my mouth

hung open about four inches wide, zillions of theories zoomed through my brain.

I was at the wrong house.

The Boy was at the wrong house.

I was hallucinating.

I had not actually been offered the job. The Boy had.

I had been struck in the head by a blunt object and was unconscious.

I was suffering from spontaneous visual impairment.

I had been sucked into the space-time continuum and whisked into hyperspace at warp speed and instantly transported to a far-reaching quadrant of space containing a universe where dreams really did come true.

"Hi," said The Boy.

"Phletamgah," I said.

What? What? What?

"What?" asked The Boy.

"Yes," I said.

At least "yes" was a word.

"So are you Lily?"

I didn't know which was better at the moment—that I was Lily, or that I'd never heard of the broad. Honesty. Honesty.

"I am Lily," I said. I sounded like the monarch of an alien world greeting throngs of humanity on an initial mission of intergalactic goodwill.

Maybe I should have stuck with "phletamgah."

"Yeah, okay," The Boy said. "You better come in. My mother isn't home yet."

"Who?" I asked. Did he want me to meet his mother? Did he mean come into the house? This house? Was I being punk'd on hidden camera for MTV?

The Boy looked at me like I might be a moron, which, to be fair, I clearly was.

"My mother? Ellis Parson? She said you were supposed to be working for her. Unless you'd rather wait outside."

"No!" I said. (I might have said it a little loudly. I might have shouted it. Oh, Dear Readers, I accidentally shouted at my One True Love.)

"No, you don't want to come in, or no, you don't—"

"I'll come in, thanks," I said.

I had tanked. I had come face-to-face with The Boy after hours of studying *Rock & Ice*, and I had tanked. Blown my only chance at happiness. It was all over now. There was nothing to do but crawl under a bush and wither away.

"Lemonade? Soda?" The Boy said as I slithered shamefully into the house. "She said to get you something to drink."

Wait—I knew the answer to this one.

"Yes, please," I said. Then added, "Lemonade would be great."

Pippi Longstocking would have come off more glamorous than me at that moment. And *exotic*? Forget it. *Neurotic* was more like it.

"You want to wait in the office?" The Boy asked. He was already walking toward the kitchen. I walked over to the office, peered inside.

Suddenly something he'd said hit me.

Ellis wasn't home yet.

Wasn't home.

Wasn't here.

I was alone with The Boy.

What had happened to punctuality? How had I gone from warming up my fingers for typing to finding myself at a house, with absolutely no dignity available, with The Boy? I had to organize these new facts. Okay, Ellis was his mother. Divorced, so that explained the different last names. The Boy lived here. I might have been able to work with that, if I'd been prepared. But I was not prepared. Why did he have to be here now? Shouldn't he be at track-and-field practice or climbing in the Gumbs or something?

No, I was not ready for this.

I went into the office and sat on the stool Ellis had offered me at the interview. I had a brief but crazy thought that I was sitting on a Tibetan yak-milking stool that Bonnie had brought Ellis as a gift—that in fact everyone

61

in school knew Ellis and there was a constant stream of students going in and out of her house, and that if I went into the bathroom or peeked upstairs, I'd see other people I knew, or wanted to know, or needed to avoid.

I heard footsteps. I sat up straight, but not so straight that it would look like I was trying to sit up straight. I fluffed my hair a little, regretted it, and smoothed it back.

The Boy came into the office with a glass of lemonade.

HE WAS MAGNIFICENT! He was tall enough to be kind of a big guy without actually dwarfing anyone. A piece of perfectly straight red hair fell forward over one eyebrow. His eyes were as blue as . . . as blue as . . . well, I didn't have TIME for adjectives. His expression was serene and intelligent. His jeans were faded almost white and worn clear through at one knee. He wore crimson Converse hightops. I wanted to take those sneakers home and build a shrine around them. It was possible I was beginning to hear that music again.

He was a Poem. The Boy was a Poem.

"So do you want to take this?" The Boy asked, still holding out the glass.

I reached for the lemonade. Yes, the Boy was a Poem, and I was the recipe for Doofus Pie.

"So she ought to be back soon, but she's always late. For everything."

"Right," I said. "I mean, who?"

Now The Boy really did look at me with concern, like I was a puppy that kept meowing.

"My mother," he said. "Ellis Parson? You *are* Lily who's supposed to be working for her, right?"

Oh, boy. This guy was NEVER going to marry me now.

"Yeah! I'm sorry, I'm just a little spaced. . . . You know, this is my first day working for Ellis, and I thought—"

"Whatever. You'll have to get used to her—she's never where she's supposed to be. She can't keep track of her own head." The Boy looked around like he was seeing the office for the first time.

"I guess that's why she needs an assistant," I said. Hey, that wasn't bad, conversational-wise.

"I guess," The Boy said, apparently not impressed with my banter.

Should I bring up climbing, or was it too soon? Should I wait until I had studied more, until I knew what rap bolting actually was? It might be my last chance to impress him, but then again, if I brought up climbing first, having no legitimate reason to KNOW he was into climbing, he could think I was stalking him!

And that could look a mite unattractive.

"So I've really gotta go," The Boy said.

Oh.

"Sure," I said. "Of course! I've got homework." I

reached over and patted my book bag.

He may have given me a look that indicated only losers did homework. Or maybe he just had a gas bubble and swallowed the burp to be polite. I wasn't sure of ANY-THING anymore.

"Yeah, whatever. The bathroom's through there, if you need it," said The Boy.

I found it unnecessarily humiliating for The Boy to be making reference to potential bodily functions at this point.

"Thanks," I said.

"Catch you later."

I sincerely doubted that.

And then The Boy was gone.

How long did Romeo and Juliet have before fate wrenched them apart? How long did Rhett and Scarlett have before their love was Gone with the Wind? Even Leo DiCaprio and Kate Winslet had a week or so before the *Titanic* sank.

My lackluster ten minutes with The Boy flew in the face of everything that was conventional and acceptable in the Literature of Love.

I had been ripped off. Left in the lurch. An old maid at barely fourteen.

In the distance, the front door closed.

The house was now as quiet as a tomb. (Okay, I've

never actually spent any time inside a tomb, but give me a little poetic license here.) There wasn't even a clock ticking. No traffic sounds outside. No tinny sounds of a radio playing in the distance. It was completely silent. I had been sucked into the Silent Vortex of Despair.

The phone rang. I jumped straight up into the air with a little startled shriek and waited to see if I was going into full cardiac arrest.

I could not have felt more fear at that moment if I had come face-to-face with the guy in the hockey mask who stars in all those movies. Was this a test? Should I answer it? Would answering it be absolutely the right thing to do? Or would it get me fired? It might be thoroughly wrong to presume to answer someone else's phone. But then again, I was supposed to be Ellis's assistant. But then again, I hadn't actually started assisting anything. Maybe I should just let it ring.

Maybe it was Ellis calling me.

Maybe it was for The Boy.

Maybe the machine would get it, and I could screen the call.

The phone stopped ringing.

Okay. Okay. So that happened.

Except I heard something else now. A noise I could not identify. A clicking sound, in a certain kind of rhythm, growing louder. *Clickety-clickety-clickety.* Like the sound that might be made from a tiny typewriter, no bigger than a Twinkie. It was coming closer. Then it stopped. I turned, slowly, to the doorway.

It was a beagle.

I laughed out loud with relief.

"Hey, little guy!" I said.

The beagle seemed to smile with his ears (you have to really look at a beagle to understand how this is possible).

"Hey!" I repeated. "Come here, buddy!"

The beagle obligingly trotted forward, his doggy toenails click-clicking on the floor. His tail wagged energetically, and when he reached me, he made himself into a little U shape, offering me his back to scratch while bending his head around to face me at the same time.

"Good boy, buddy," I said, scratching his back and smiling into his enormous brown eyes. "That's nice, isn't it?"

The beagle smiled and wagged and stretched his U shape and made little piggy sounds, grunting and oinking with pleasure.

I suddenly felt okay. Bonnie would say that this was a message from The Universe that everything was all right. This little manifestation of beagle happiness was a sign to reassure me, to calm me, to reinstate my optimism.

The beagle made another funny sound in his throat, then a deeper one that seemed to come from his stomach.

He straightened his U shape into a regular dog shape and took a step back. His stomach made the noise again. He looked like someone was tugging his head forward.

"Are you okay there, buddy?" I asked, growing mildly alarmed.

The beagle continued to make strange, hiccupy movements. He seemed to lurch slightly to one side. Then suddenly his head jutted forward and he threw up a little ball of grass onto the floor. When it was out, the beagle's knees buckled, and he keeled over onto his back, all four paws in the air.

I had killed Ellis Parson's dog.

Five

About five seconds into my getting used to the fact that I'd killed Ellis Parson's dog, the beagle gave a little twitch, yawned, and rolled to his feet as if nothing unusual had happened. He gave his vomited grass ball a little sniff, cast an apologetic look in my direction, and trotted back out of the room.

My first day as a Real Writer's assistant, and all I had accomplished was embarrassing myself in front of The Boy I wished to marry and inspiring a beagle to lose both his lunch and his consciousness. I reached up to touch Bonnie's necklace, running my fingers over the ancient glass. Maybe the necklace was cursed. No, passing cursed jewelry along to people definitely wasn't Bonnie's style. Maybe the necklace just didn't like me. Then again, maybe the necklace adored me, and if I had not been wearing it, things would have been much worse. For example, it might have been me throwing up that grass ball on The Boy. Now THAT was something to consider.

Where was Ellis? Was I going to get paid for today? I unzipped my book bag and rummaged around in it. Homework seemed too complicated—I didn't want to start anything and have books and notes spread all over the place IF Ellis finally came in. I had The Boy Pages, but I couldn't possibly write about The Boy while sitting in his house. That was too weird even for me.

Thinking about the fact that I was in The Boy's home brought me to the sudden realization that somewhere, probably upstairs, was his room. His ROOM with the closet where his crimson Converse sneakers rested when he wasn't wearing them; the bed with the pillow he rested his head on at night; his clothes, his CDs—I was mere steps away from a MAJOR TROVE OF BOY PARA-PHERNALIA! If there had been a pair of handcuffs lying around, I would have locked myself to Ellis's desk to phys-ically prevent myself from sneaking upstairs. For just one peek. I wouldn't even actually have to go in. I could simply stand in the doorway and absorb details. . . .

Then I had a sudden flash of Charlotte's and Bonnie's faces, sort of floating free form in my frontal lobe. Charlotte would be horrified at the lack of professionalism implicit in departing my designated employee work space without authorization. Bonnie would gravely point out the hazards of violating the personal space of another human being without his or her consent.

"All right!" I hissed at the phantom faces of my buddies. Either I was having a genuine psychic experience based on deep-seated past-life bonds, or I was as crazy as an overbaked nut loaf. Either way, I was now firmly resolved to resist temptation and remain exactly where I was. I would have to keep busy some other way.

I had one Lily Pad letter that I hadn't answered yet. Cautiously I looked out the office window that faced the street and the driveway. No sign of a car anywhere. Maybe it was unethical to do Lily Pad work in Ellis Parson's office, but I had to do something. I unfolded the letter.

Dear Lily,

    I've read some of the answers you've put in to peoples letters. What I want to know is, what makes you so special? Everyone has problems and you write them all back like you know everything and you are so above it all and we all should listen to you because you're like Yoda from STAR WARS or something—yeah, you do kind of look like him, now that you mention it.

    Why should anyone listen to what you say?

               Challenging Chick

I'm ashamed to say it, Dear Readers, but this letter brought tears to my eyes, and I do not mean that in a touched, romantic-comedy Hilary Duff kind of way. I mean it in an angry, defensive, increasingly paranoid way. Why would someone send me a stupid letter like this? And how was it fair that Challenging Chick got to know who I was, and she got to hide behind a stupid, advice-seeking nickname? Were people laughing at me and the Lily Pad? And I did not look a thing like Yoda! All right, I was a little on the short side, and more than one hair-dresser had told me I had a round face. But any fool could see I wasn't green! I had hair! My ears didn't point or stick out! I did not wear sacking and walk with a cane!

I grabbed my pen and notebook. My first instinct had been to throw the letter away and forget about it. But no, that wouldn't do. I was going to answer this letter. And I wasn't going to rip Challenging to shreds, as I was ca-pable of doing in a cutthroat, big-city theater critic kind of a way. Dignity with an edge. That's what I'd have. Challenging hadn't offered a problem of her own, but she didn't need to. Her work was a minefield of grammatical blunders. I opened my notebook and began to write.

Dear Challenging,
   To begin with, let's take a look at YOUR letter, shall we? Sentence No. 1—I have not put any answers into people's (possessive form requires apostrophe) letters,

as you say. I publish responses in our school newspaper to submitted queries. Sentence No. 2—gratuitous use of comma after the word "is." Sentence No. 3 indicates that I have written to everyone's problems. Clearly, this is inaccurate. I write to people, not problems. Nor do I request that anyone listen to what I say, since, as you may have noticed, the Lily Pad is not a talk show, it is a printed advice column. Yoda is a copyrighted character and I will not infringe on that protection by further incorporating him into this published response.

Lastly, Challenging, I am special for the same reason that you are special. I leave you to extract the meaning in that statement yourself. And for the record, I write this column because I was asked to by the editors of this publication, who are possibly aware of my perspicacious nature and my Brobdingnagian stores of compassion.

Write again if you really need help, Challenging, and I'll do my best.

Grammatically yours,
Lily M. Blennerhassett

I sat rereading my letter with a small sense of satisfaction. I'd as good as guaranteed that Challenging would have to run to the dictionary at least twice, if for no other reason than to ensure she was not being insulted. I began to feel very good. How many writers, after all, get to use the words "perspicacious" and "Brobdingnagian" in the SAME sentence?

The front door slammed, and I snapped my notebook closed and jumped to my feet. Was it Her? Was it Him? It wouldn't be Him. It must be Her. I probably looked anxious just standing there the way I was, so I sat back down again. Crossed my legs. Recrossed them the other way. Thought of the faraway look Bonnie got when she was about to go OOBE and tried to make the same face myself.

I hadn't noticed footsteps, but Ellis Parson herself was coming into the office. I breathed a sigh of relief that she was finally here, and I noticed with a tiny thrill that she was wearing a Mexican embroidered tunic shirt and shiny silver earrings—a sun on one ear, the moon on the other. Did the Jumble Trunk sell Mexican tunics?

"Lily, darling, I'm so sorry I'm late," Ellis said breathlessly, as if she'd just jogged all the way down the interstate from New Hampshire. "Have you been waiting long?"

It was four fifteen. I'd been waiting forty-five minutes. To admit this would be like pointing out to Ellis how very, very, very late she was. To say that no, I had *not* been waiting long might make it sound like I had waltzed in a half hour late myself. I was rescued from this dilemma when I noticed that the little ball of beagle vomit was still resting peacefully on the middle of the floor.

"Oh, be careful," I said, pointing. "The beagle . . ."

Ellis immediately saw what I was pointing at.

"Oh, that Milo," she said. "It's a good thing he's so cute."

She grabbed a tissue from the box on her desk, scooped up the little ball, and tossed it into the garbage.

"Maybe he needs to go to the vet," I said.

Ellis tossed her purse onto a shelf piled high with reference books.

"Oh, no, Milo throws up all the time," she said. "It's a beagle thing. You get used to it."

"Well, the thing is, Ellis, that isn't all he did," I offered nervously. Maybe I should have called the vet myself. Maybe Milo had simply left the room to die alone!

Ellis froze, then looked around.

"Did he puddle?" she asked.

Puddle? A published writer and alleged expert on medieval England wanted to know if her dog had "puddled"?

"He keeled over," I said. And I did nothing about it, did not alert the veterinary authorities, I added silently. Now I was going to get fired. I was going to lose my job.

But Ellis just laughed.

"Believe it or not, he does that all the time, too. He

works so hard throwing up that he forgets to breathe; then he faints. We call him Milo the Fainting Dog. It's a little embarrassing. He's also afraid of ironing boards. Now, let's see what we have for you to do."

Relieved, I drew myself up to my full five feet three and a half inches, ready to receive my assignment. Then Ellis's phone rang. She answered it, holding up one finger in the Charlotte McGrath "wait and do not speak" signal. Well trained, I waited.

I waited.

I waited.

Ellis was on the phone for a good ten minutes. Eleven minutes, to be precise, because I checked the time. She was talking about artwork for a paperback edition of one of her books.

"Trixie, has the illustrator actually *read* the book?" Ellis exclaimed, sounding exasperated.

Trixie must have responded inadequately, because Ellis kept repeating the question.

I was trying to appear as if I wasn't listening, but I just couldn't help myself. Here was an actual Publishing Conversation taking place, the very kind I myself intended to have with someone named Trixie one day. While soaking up every word, I tried to look disinterested but not bored, so Ellis think I was professional, but not starstruck. That was when Ellis caught my eye. She pointed at the telephone, rolled her eyes, then began to move her lips in the International Symbol for blah-blah-blah-blahbetty-blah-blah. I laughed, and Ellis smiled brightly at me, her eyes glittering.

"Listen, Trix, my new assistant is here, and between my senior moments with getting places on time and your phone call, I've kept her waiting for the better part of an hour. Just deal with it, okay? Tell them to get the illustrator who does the Sharon Kay Penman books. At least he reads the book before he draws the cover."

I clasped my hands together with a feeling of anticipation. Ellis and I were suddenly a team, bonding in the face of Trixie's overtalking.

"Okay, okay," Ellis said. "E-mail me a JPEG of the sketch. 'Bye."

She hung up, gave a huge sigh, and stared at me with humorous exasperation.

"How they expect me to write on top of everything else I need to take care of, I simply do not know," Ellis said. She smiled at me. She had a white T-shirt under her Mexican tunic and faded cream-colored leggings rolled up at the bottom. She had brushed her short hair straight up so that it looked almost like a crew cut, but nothing could look too military with those celestial earrings.

Ellis Parson had style.

"What I want to know," she continued, plopping down

in the chair by her desk and kicking off her hemp sandals, "is how people who have children find time to write."

No children? No rock-climbing son? Had I HALLU-CINATED the entire Boy Episode? Dear Readers, I needed to be institutionalized IMMEDIATELY!

"Little children, of course, I mean," Ellis added, before I could fully picture myself wearing a straitjacket. "When kids hit fifteen, their parents turn into these useless appendages. Which reminds me, did you meet Colter? He just started ninth grade at your school. A year ahead of you, I guess. I'm surprised you didn't run into him on your way in."

"Oh, no," I said. "I mean, YES." Which sounded stupid. Which made me stupid. Again. But Ellis didn't seem to notice. Oh, good—she was the kind of writer who usually occupied a parallel universe, emerging only occasionally to participate in her side of a conversation. Or drive. I had read about writers like this. I liked them. I wanted to be the same way. Like Bonnie, but off in the book world instead of the spirit world. But for now one of us had to be in THIS Universe, and since Ellis was the Real Writer and I was the Assistant, I had to stay firmly within the confines of Einstein's space-time continuum.

"Anyway," Ellis said, running one hand through her hair until it stuck up even more. "Let me think. Where am I? What am I doing?"

I waited patiently.

"Did we talk about what I'm working on? I'm just beginning the second chapter of a novel about Eleanor of Aquitaine," Ellis said. "English, twelfth century. Do you know the story? She was married to Henry II, the father of Richard the Lionheart and King John. And before that she was married to the king of France, Louis VII. Imagine that, married to two kings, and mother to two kings. Henry eventually had her locked up."

I nodded, listening intently and praying to every higher power I knew that Ellis wouldn't ask me any questions.

"Did you ever see the movie *The Lion in Winter*?" she asked.

Rats! I thought I had seen everything! Could it be a sequel to *The Lion King*? Better not venture a guess. I shook my head.

"Shame. You'll have to rent it. Actually, I have it. I'll lend it to you. Peter O'Toole plays Henry II, and Katharine Hepburn, *Katharine Hepburn*, plays Eleanor. Can you imagine? Oh, no, oh, please, *please* don't tell me you don't know who Katharine Hepburn is . . ."

"Oh, of course I do!" I said, thrilled to be having this honest and reassuring moment. My mother did painful imitations of Katharine Hepburn on a regular basis.

"Good. What a relief. I know I'm old and out of date, but some things I insist must endure, and Katharine

Hepburn is one of them. So Eleanor. I'm picking up the story after Eleanor's marriage to Louis is annulled but before she marries Henry," Ellis said. "The part where Henry's brother, Geoffrey, tries to kidnap Eleanor so he can force her into marriage himself."

"For real?" I said. I was trying to look interested in what she was saying, which was becoming complicated as I now actually WAS interested in what she was saying.

"For real," said Ellis,

Whoa.

"That kind of thing happened a lot in those days. Pounce on an heiress traveling through the countryside, drag her to a priest, and marry her at swordpoint. Boom. You're instantly a rich and landed man. That wouldn't go over so well in this day and age. So you see, we have made some progress in the battle of the sexes."

"I'll say," I replied.

"Anyway, that's what I'm working on right now," Ellis said. "I'm a little scattered today. There's so much I need to do. I'm trying to think how you can best help me right now. Give me a moment."

I imagined Ellis sending me to the dark, musty basement of an organization that housed rare medieval historical reference works. I would sit in a quiet, cell-like room, hundreds of ancient books piled on a thick oak table before me. I would scour each book for descriptions of

Geoffrey's abduction of Eleanor. The date, the time, the weather. I would find an old, obscure text that detailed Eleanor's dress, her hair, her jewelry. I would discover a heretofore forgotten account of Geoffrey's squire, his unwilling help in the attempted abduction. I would copy every passage down neatly and accurately on index cards, meticulously noting each source, the author, the year of publication. I would organize the index cards according to theme, and arrange for cross-referencing according to source date. I would emerge from the room, smelling faintly of old books, my bag bulging with painstakingly collected historical detail. I would present the cards to Ellis, who would devour them as a starving man would tear into a steak. She would read the cards breathlessly, one by one, exclaiming with delight or astonishment. Then she would pause to give me a look of incredulous respect before turning to her computer and typing at lightning speed.

"What I could really use . . ." said Ellis, then her voice trailed off momentarily. I leaned forward expectantly. Ellis blinked and started again.

"What I could really use," she repeated as I began to bestow on her a brilliant smile, "is one of those tall iced coffees from the Starbucks on the corner."

Six

♡ LILY'S FANTASY INTERLUDE NUMBER TWO ♡

Lily presses the headphones closer to her ears, shuts her eyes, and begins to sway to the music. In the control room through the glass wall, the producer watches her carefully as the sound engineer makes several adjustments to the mixing board. The control room door opens, and The Boy walks in, a messenger bag slung over his shoulder. He hands an envelope to the producer, along with a clipboard to sign for the delivery. The Boy is about to put his clipboard back in his bag when he catches sight of Lily through the glass.

It is at this moment that Lily begins to sing. Everyone in the control room falls silent as Lily's voice rises, impossibly clear and richly transcendent. She sings with her eyes still closed, one hand fluttering through the air with the grace of a dancer, the other tucked into the waist of her faded low-rise jeans. She taps a stiletto heel on the floor, oblivious to everything but the music she is making. The Boy watches, utterly enraptured. Never in his life has he heard a voice so pure, a talent so explosively awe-inspiring. His knees go weak with the sheer emotion of it.

"Where did you find this girl?" asks the sound engineer, gazing reverently through the glass at Lily.

"Heard her singing to herself outside the library one day," the producer replies. "I knew then and there she was an absolutely unique talent. This girl is going to be a major, major star."

"No doubt!" says the sound engineer, grooving to the Lily beat.

Lily finishes her song, slips off the headphones, and slowly opens her eyes. She is looking straight at The Boy, and the intense gaze of her cinnamon eyes takes his breath away.

"Who are you?" he mouths.

"I am Lily," she replies, dazzling him with a smile. "Lily Blennerhassett."

The producer notices the messenger is still in the control room.

"You'll have to leave now, son," he says to The Boy.

"Wait!" The Boy cries. "Just let me talk to her for a second!"

"Sorry, kid. No one can bother the star while she's working."

"Just a second!" The Boy cries, but the producer is leading him toward the door. The Boy turns desperately in Lily's direction and shouts, "How about dinner and a movie?"

Lily's answer is apparent in her enchanting smile.

Charlotte, Bonnie, and I were sitting on the steps outside the local library, which didn't open on Saturdays until ten A.M. I was holding court, trumpeting the news of my blazing failure to accomplish anything important at yesterday's first day on the job.

"Lily," Charlotte said patiently and with considerable sympathy, "you can't let this get you down. I can think of very few business venues in which a new employee can come in and jump into meaningful work with both feet. On my first day interning with McCord, Chabon & List, I didn't do anything even remotely corporate. They weren't ready for me, they didn't know where to put me, there was no pile of work for me to do."

"So you retyped and reorganized their Rolodex on your own," I reminded her.

Charlotte was honest enough to look a little proud.

"Yes, I did do that. Mr. List said he'd never seen that kind of initiative in a summer intern."

"Well, I couldn't do something like that, Charlotte," I said. "I was in her house. She's not a business, she's a person. I couldn't start rooting around in her stuff.

Reorganizing her silverware drawer."

"I know, I know, Lily. You didn't do anything wrong."

But all the same, I knew that if Charlotte had been the one with forty-five minutes to kill in Ellis Parson's office, she would have found something to do. She would have figured out a way to make the computer run faster or programmed speed-dial numbers into the telephone. Or reviewed Ellis's tax returns and corrected errors.

"What about you, Bonnie?" I asked. "Do you have an after-school job?"

Bonnie nodded, her feather earrings bobbing gently. "I work some afternoons up at Sonia's Organic Vegetable Farm if the weather's good," she said. "I started last summer."

"What was your first day like?" I asked.

Bonnie stared off in the distance.

She's going OOBE, I thought. Her consciousness is flitting through the astral plane, connected to her body on these steps by a translucent silver cord.

"Bonnie?" I asked.

She blinked and looked over at me like I'd just spontaneously materialized in front of her.

"Sorry, bro," she said. "Where was I?"

"I think you were hovering up by that maple tree, the one—"

"No, I mean where was I in the conversation?" Bonnie asked.

"Your first day at the organic vegetable farm," Charlotte said. She wasn't completely comfortable yet with Bonnie's astral stuff. Not only was it very noncorporate, it was by its very nature nonCORPOREAL, and Charlotte only related to stuff that directly involved the human body and brain and preferably publicly traded stock options.

"Right. Well, it was really hot that day. I knew the farm, because my family's always bought all their produce there, but I couldn't find Sonia to save my life. She wasn't in the greenhouse, or in the store, or with the tomatoes or the asparagus or the beets or the potatoes—"

"So what did you do?" I asked.

"Oh, man, it was really stupid," Bonnie said. "I kept wandering up and down the fields, and I hadn't brought any water and the sun was blazing and it was getting hotter and hotter, and I finally ended up getting dizzy and passing out by the fertilizer pile just as Sonia was coming to find me. So that was my first day, man, unconscious by the cow poo."

"That's fantastic!" I shouted.

"Lily," said Charlotte reproachfully. But Bonnie gave me one of her wide, sleepy smiles.

"It *was* fantastic, man. I was right down there in that fertilizer. My molecules vibrating against its molecules, and my consciousness just fizzling away in some nonphysical place. It totally had to happen that way—I could see it almost immediately. By the time I came to and Sonia gave me some cold water, I had, like, bonded with that fertilizer. And that's where it all starts, man. Growth starts with fertilizer. It's the cycle of life, its most basic symbol. I became the earth and the growth and the life at that moment. Made me a great gardener."

Only Bonnie could fall into a pile of crap and find a life lesson. I admired that. I truly, truly did.

"Are we actually going into the library?" Charlotte asked. Another Abrupt Subject Change. Vibrating molecules and bonding weren't her thing either.

"Not me," Bonnie said. "I've got plans—I was gonna ask you guys if you wanted to come along."

"What did you have in mind?" I asked while already reviewing excuses. Bonnie's plans could easily involve sitting cross-legged at the lake and contemplating its emptiness for an hour or two.

"My big bro Jake found a local face he wants to try a little top roping on, work out a route," Bonnie said.

Wait. Were these CLIMBING words? Was she talking about climbing?

"He's meeting that guy you were talking about, Colter, by the lake. We don't have any gear, I know, but we could watch, maybe get on belay if we can poach a harness."

My heart began pounding so hard, I expected the

boinging to be visible through my shirt, like in a Warner Bros. cartoon.

A chance to go climbing. Or be present while others climbed. With The Boy.

Suddenly I knew Charlotte was going to say no. Charlotte DID want to go into the library. She wanted to study and peruse international news publications. Charlotte liked to spend her downtime seeking brain fun indoors. She did not like to visit nature for pleasure. She did not like bugs. She did not like sun. She did not like places without furniture. She certainly was not going to be interested in anything even remotely related to rock climbing.

Dear Readers, I COULD NOT PERMIT HER TO SAY NO! The cardinal rule of Obtaining Proximity to a Likable Boy was that Charlotte and I had to stick together. Bonnie would be there, true, and I liked Bonnie, but she was liable to start sketching or meditating or slipping out of her body. I needed backup, reliable, trustworthy, and consistent.

"Charlotte and I definitely want to go," I said. Then I slapped Charlotte discreetly on the side of the leg, telling her that yes, she WOULD go in spite of the fact that she didn't WANT to because it was a crucial watershed moment in MY LIFE and I required the presence and support of my oldest and best FRIEND. That it would be made up to her in some way at some point in the future, but that she must accompany me NOW.

Charlotte sighed so heavily, I swear I saw a stop sign on the corner bend under its force. (Well, no, Dear Readers, I don't actually swear I saw that. Hyperbole—a tool of the trade.) I hastily got to my feet.

"So now? Now would be a good time? We go now to the lake?"

How did I manage to sound like an English-language instruction audiotape without even trying?

"No time like the present, dude," Bonnie said. "If we cut through the woods, we'll be there in ten minutes."

I could feel Charlotte's scowl burrowing into my back like a pair of rabid leeches. I whirled around, grabbed her hand, beamed a sunshiny smile, and led her behind Bonnie.

"You owe me," she whispered, just loudly enough for me to hear.

And I did. I knew that I did. And I'd pay her back, too. No matter how things eventually turned out.

When we got to the lake, The Boy and Jake were already in action. I caught my breath.

The Boy was a good twenty feet up the crag. Since his back was to me and he was a little busy, I was free to stare at him all I liked. He was wearing a yellow T-shirt and a pair of black close-cut pants that looked made for climb-ing. He had on a white helmet and a pair of slippers that looked like ballet shoes. (NEVER let him know I said that, Dear Readers.) He had a harness around his legs and hips, and a rope extended from him to the top of the crag and back down to the ground, where Bonnie's brother Jake was holding the free end tight and watching The Boy's every move.

I had never seen anything like it. Twenty feet may not seem that high to you. But go outside, find a big rock, measure twenty feet up, then picture The Boy Who Is the Center of Your Universe clinging to that place, looking resplendent in climbing shoes. Then you'll know what I mean.

"Unbelievable," said Charlotte from beside me.

Jake glanced over his shoulder at us.

"Hey, Bonnie. Hey, Bonnie's friends. I was right! This place is perfect for top roping!" Jake called, then turned his attention back to The Boy. Jake, with all his similari-ties in Bonnie's pale, delicate coloring, was not a bad-looking boy. Not a bad-looking boy at all. But my attention was elsewhere.

I watched The Boy like a hawk.

He was only about eight feet from the top now. He clung to the rock with both hands as he lifted his right foot up the wall and brushed it, feeling for a hold. Then he shifted his weight, pushed up, and raised himself another foot up the wall. His hands seemed to find holds like he already knew where they were. Resting for a moment, he reached one hand behind him and dipped it into a little bag clipped to his harness. At first I thought maybe he had a little snack back there, you know, to keep his energy up. But when he pulled out his hand, a little white cloud poofed out into the air, and I remembered reading that climbers carried chalk bags to keep their grip from slipping. The thought of The Boy slipping made my eyeballs bulge in terror (at least, Dear Readers, I like to think so).

"What if he falls?" I asked Bonnie. Okay, kind of a numbskull question, but be real—aren't YOU curious, too?

"He's on belay," Bonnie said. Before I could ask her what this nifty-sounding word meant (and I wanted to say it—I wanted to tell someone that I was "on belay,") she continued.

"They're top roping. They built an anchor up at the top of the crag," Bonnie said. "Colter ties one end of the rope to his harness. The rope goes up and loops through the anchor and back down to the ground—Jake is holding that end tight with a little gizmo that won't let the rope slip unless he undoes the brake. Every time Colter moves up the rock, Jake pulls the rope tight so there's no slack. If he falls, he'll just hang there until he can get himself back on the rock again."

Incredible. LOVE should be that easy. Risk-free falling!

The Boy had reached the top and scrambled up to his feet.

"Slack!" he called down. He moved about ten feet to his left, then knelt down and started working with his hands. He looked like he was building a sand castle, all recreational and contemplative.

"What's he doing?" Charlotte asked.

Bless her, she was paying attention.

"He's setting a second anchor for an easier climb," said Jake, turning to face us for the first time now that his belaying duties were temporarily suspended. He gave me a charming grin. Oh, for The Boy to give me such a grin. "Hey, y'all. I'm Jake."

Neither Jake nor Bonnie was southern, but the y'all sounded warm and comfortable when Jake said it. Like one of Bonnie's bros or mans. I instantly felt more relaxed.

"Charlotte and Lily," Bonnie said, correctly identifying each of us by pointing.

"Welcome to the climb," Jake said.

"Are you going up?" Bonnie asked.

"Already been twice," Jake said. "We started with some easy routes, then flashed a tough one—I'd say that last one was a five-point-ten."

Yet more lingo I didn't understand. I'd look up "flashed" and "five-point-ten" later. Right now, something was happening on the top of the rock. The Boy was peering down over the edge at Jake.

"Take! And lower!" called The Boy.

"Take?" Charlotte asked.

"And lower?" I added, to make sure Jake knew I was in on the game. Whatever the game was.

"He's finished building the directional anchor, so I'm going to lower him back down."

As Jake let out the rope, The Boy came slowly toward the ground. Oh, Dear Readers, it was like Adonis descending from Mount Olympus. Or any Greek God reference you prefer. He was . . . DIVINE. As his feet neared the ground, I instantly became Lily Blennerhasset, Grape Jelly Girl. Wibbly Wobbly. Probably sweet, but not much help without white bread and peanut butter.

"That was excellent," The Boy was saying enthusiastically to Jake. "There are some awesome holds. Did you see my heel hook? If we move the anchor over around ten feet, I think we can work that roof into a route."

I just stood and stared, grape jelly on legs.

"Better you than me, man," Jake said. "I don't think I can pull that roof. Hey, these are Bonnie's friends, Charlotte and Lily."

The Boy turned and nodded at us. He graced me with a classic double take.

"We met yesterday at your mother's," I said quickly.

"Right," he said. Like maybe he'd been hoping to forget about it. Like he was wondering how a Grape Jelly Girl ended up at his climb.

Okay, Dear Readers. I realize I'm giving you the impression that I have no self-confidence whatsoever, and that is not true. I am Lily Blennerhassett. I dispense advice professionally. I have an unusual predilection for all things written and verbal. I am going to be a successful and highly emulated writer. I am an excellent student. I am generally liked and perhaps, in some scholastic circles, admired. I do not detest my thighs, and my eyes have been (okay, by my mother) compared to Julia Roberts's. I am a work in progress, and the prognosis is good. You see? I am not one of those girls who hate themselves and think everything is hopeless.

"I take it the girls don't climb?" The Boy asked, glancing toward me, then away again.

I hate myself and everything is hopeless.

"Maybe they want to try," Jake says. "I've been teaching Bonnie some moves. She knows how to belay. What about it, Bonnie's friends? Either one of you want to give it a shot?"

It was kind of nice of him to make it sound like he actually wanted to teach two novice girls how to climb. But The Boy looked impatient. We would slow him down, take away from his climbing time. I knew right away this was the WRONG time for me to investigate a new sport. Lily and Charlotte would not climb.

There were several different ways for us to say no. Charlotte, of course, would simply be blunt and say it wasn't her thing. Charlotte wasn't one to stand on ceremony. Charlotte wasn't the kind of person to get pressured into trying something she clearly did not and could not do. She was a future business executive, not an athlete. I'd let Charlotte say no first, then I'd make it sound like I wasn't going to do it because Charlotte wasn't going to do it.

"Sure, I'll try it," Charlotte said.

For the second time in two days I wondered briefly if I had been hit on the head and become delusional. Was this a joke? Had Bonnie and Charlotte planned this entire prank earlier just for a laugh?

But Jake was pulling out a spare harness from his gear bag and showing Charlotte how to put it on. The Boy sighed. Maybe it was impatience. Maybe he was just tuckered out from his workout.

Charlotte in a climbing harness? That was like picturing Brad Pitt in a tutu—it simply did not compute.

"And you've got to make sure it's really snug," Jake was saying. Charlotte's fingers were working the buckles like she'd been training for this moment all year.

WHAT IN THE NAME OF JANE AUSTEN WAS GOING ON HERE?

"This is awesome, Charlotte!" Bonnie cried. "I can't believe you're going up—this is just so RIGHTEOUS!"

Righteous was not the word I was searching for.

"You can't go without a brain bucket," Jake said. "We've been sharing the one. Can she wear it, bro?"

The Boy hesitated a moment, then took off his helmet and handed it to Jake.

"It adjusts," said Jake. "I'm going to make it a little smaller."

Charlotte stood patiently as Jake fastened The Boy's helmet onto her head. It wasn't fair! I should be wearing The Boy's brain bucket! That brain bucket rightfully belonged on me!

"Now we tie you in," said Jake, knotting the rope through Charlotte's harness.

"See that long crack going up the rock?" Jake asked, gesturing at the crag. "Go up on the left side of it. That's an easy climb, probably a five-point-three or so. Relax and go with it. Feel for holds, move up when you're confident you've got a good one. Don't worry about falling, because I'll have you on a tight belay. You can't go anywhere—you'll just swing. And anytime you want to come down, say the word and I'll lower you. No worries. You're going to love this, you'll see."

"Okay," said Charlotte. She stood and looked up the crag for a moment.

Now the full realization of what she's gotten into is

hitting her, I thought. Maybe she had just been trying to take the pressure off me by volunteering to climb so I didn't have to say no. Poor Charlotte. Now she had all this stuff on, and the guys were looking at her and waiting for her to do something when she and I both knew she couldn't stand physical exertion whatsoever, hated heights, and had in fact once gotten sick on the Dumbo ride at Disneyland. She was going to wait one minute, then admit she couldn't do it. Admit she was in fact scared stiff, as I knew she must be. Charlotte was sacrificing her dignity in the name of friendship so that I would not have to embarrass myself in front of The Boy. She was a saint. She was the best friend a girl could ever dream of having.

Charlotte took a step forward, put both her hands and one foot on the wall, and hoisted herself up. Jake stood steadily at the base of the rock, both his hands on his end of the rope, which looped through a device attached to his own harness.

And then, Dear Readers, Charlotte began to climb.

The Boy stood off to one side, looking bored, which was understandable. I'd have been bored, too, if I wasn't so busy feeling a murderous rage at my best friend. Charlotte was still climbing, and gaining speed as she went.

"Whoa," said Bonnie.

"Up rope! Take up the slack," said The Boy to Jake.

"Geez, man," Jake said. "Look at her go. Bon, has she climbed before?"

"No way, dude," Bonnie said, staring at Charlotte. "She's a newbie, I swear! Isn't she, Lily?"

"She got sick on the Dumbo ride at Disneyland," I murmured.

It didn't even matter what I said. No one was paying attention to me. Certainly not The Boy. They were all watching Charlotte move smoothly up the rock face like she was Tobey Maguire's stunt double in *Spiderman*.

"Not bad," said The Boy.

"Not bad?" Jake said excitedly, never taking his attention from Charlotte and the rope. "Man, she's excellent! Like a total natural. I've never seen anyone climb like this the first time out."

"This must be a past life influence bleeding into this lifetime," Bonnie said in awe.

Great. Charlotte was a champion climber in a past life. And I had apparently spent my last life as a potted plant.

"Okay, you're almost all the way up," Jake called. "You're doing incredible, Charlotte, your climbing is awesome! Another two feet . . . that's it . . . YOU'RE THERE! Reach up and touch the anchor."

"Got it!" Charlotte called.

"Oh, man, you rock!" yelled Bonnie. I think she was

talking to Charlotte, but with Bonnie, she might actually have been talking to the cliff itself.

"Don't try to climb up and over," Jake shouted. "Just sit back into the harness, and I'll lower you."

"Okay!" Charlotte called. But before she did, she stayed there another moment, one hand gripping the crag confidently, the other resting on the anchor as she gazed around her and took in her unexpected accomplishment.

"Totally awesome," said Jake.

"Totally," agreed Bonnie.

"Not bad for a girl," admitted The Boy.

Charlotte Ascendant. Charlotte Betrayer.

I would never speak to her again.

Seven

"How could you do that?" I yelled at Charlotte.

"It was like my hands and feet just knew where to go," Charlotte said. "And my movements became all fluid and I sort of slithered up—"

"No, to ME!" I yelled. "How could you do that TO ME?"

We were walking home, fresh from the infamous climbing incident. Bonnie had stayed behind to help pack up the gear.

Charlotte stopped walking and looked at me. The sidewalk was on a quiet street, and the only sound was a car in the distance.

"Oh," Charlotte said. "I see."

"Good!" I yelled. "Wait. What do you see?"

"I see what it is that you're doing," Charlotte said.

She was going to make me drag it out of her. Fine. I had dragged things out of Charlotte McGrath before.

"What am I doing?" I shot back.

"You're interpreting everything through your own worldview," Charlotte said calmly but firmly. "You're giving all the import to yourself. No one else has any role in your dramas except to assist you. No one else is allowed to do anything for themselves. You're making it all about you, you, you."

"I am not!" I shouted, knowing full well that I was lying. Hey, I was Honest in the last chapter and I'll be Honest in the next chapter, and I'm being Honest with you now, Dear Readers, between the dialogue. It WAS about me, me, me. But I was feeling too small to be Honest with Charlotte at the moment.

"Yes, you are," Charlotte said, resuming her smooth, executivelike walk.

"Am not!" I retorted. Now I was not only lying, I was acting like a baby to boot. You see, Dear Readers? At least I know that I know.

"Lily, you make it very hard to be your friend sometimes."

Now that could have meant any number of things. It might have been about the time I gave Charlotte the chicken pox while trying to prove that she couldn't get it from sharing my soda. It might have been because I sometimes do not let her finish a sentence. There was also that little thing last summer where I said I was sleeping over at her house but I actually went to visit La Famille LeBlanc and the police came to Charlotte's house because my parents couldn't find me and thought I'd been kid-napped, and things—well—escalated. It might have been any of those things, but otherwise, I cannot imagine how ANYONE would find it hard to be my friend. Speak up, Dear Readers, if you disagree. But honestly. This is ME we're talking about.

"I have no idea what you mean," I said haughtily. Well, I *tried* to sound haughty. I'm not actually sure what a haughty person sounds like. I don't know many haughty people.

"You do know what I mean," Charlotte said, "and if you don't, you should."

"Well, you made me miss my chance with The Boy," I insisted. "There we all were, in the same zip code and everything, and suddenly you're all enthusiastic about climbing, and if that isn't enough, you have to turn out to be GOOD at it. What a disaster! You have to admit, you ruined EVERYTHING for me!"

Charlotte stopped walking again and glared at me, her hands on her hips. I'm telling you, getting the glare from the Charlotte lamps while she is simultaneously putting both her hands on her hips is a very, VERY scary thing.

"Listen to yourself!" she exclaimed. "Bonnie gave you a perfect opportunity today, taking us over to watch The Boy climb. And what did you do? Nothing. It isn't your friends' job to MAKE life happen for you, Lily. We can be there for you, and provide a little moral support, but when it comes down to the moment, YOU are the one who needs to speak. YOU are the one who needs to act. No one else can do it FOR you. And if you don't believe that being Lily Blennerhassett is good enough to impress The Boy, nothing anyone can do will change that."

I scowled, mostly because I had nothing to say. Charlotte was beginning to sound frighteningly like a person who was RIGHT, and honestly, sometimes I just hated that so much.

"As for climbing," she continued, "they asked if I wanted to try. And keeping in mind, Lily, that I've just established it is not necessary for me to stop living MY LIFE when you have something important on your personal agenda, I suddenly felt the urge to give it a try. Besides, I've read that several Fortune 500 companies take their employees on rock-climbing trips to foster teamwork and communication skills."

Ah. I knew Fortune 500 companies must figure into this somehow.

"And I decided to try it, Lily, in spite of the fact that

there was a good chance I wouldn't be able to do it, or I would be too scared. I did get sick on the Dumbo ride at Disneyland, if you remember."

Oh, yes. I remembered.

"But when I was at Young Executive Camp, they really drummed in this idea of being willing to take risks, even with the possibility of personal failure. Or humiliation. So I took a risk, and what did I find out? I CAN ROCK CLIMB! I mean, that was one of the most amazing experiences of my life. I was terrified, but I climbed anyway, and I found out that not only could I do it, but I could do it well! And here I'm having this huge life experience about overcoming fear and excelling at something, and what does my best friend have to say? She says, 'How could you do that to me?' That's what she says to MY huge life experience. She wants to know how I could do that. TO HER."

Charlotte was done. She pursed her lips for emphasis. I stared at the sidewalk. There was an ant making its way past my foot, carrying a dead ant. Why do they do that, anyway? Is there some ant funeral home they go to? Does the first ant stagger in after carrying the dead ant the human equivalent of ten miles, toss it down into the tastefully furnished hall of the ant funeral parlor, and shout, "Customer!"?

Do they send tiny flowers?

"I am wrong."

That was me speaking, Dear Readers, in case anyone was wondering.

"I am wrong, Charlotte, and you are right. I'm mad because I've come face-to-face with The Boy twice, and I have failed to make him notice me in any way. I am mad because I was afraid to try climbing, and you tried it, and you were good. I am wretched and reprehensible and opprobrious."

Charlotte peered at me through her glasses.

"What does opprobrious mean?" she asked.

"Publicly disgraced because of bad behavior," I said.

"Well, then. Yes, you are. You are wretched and reprehensible and opprobrious. And I accept your apology."

My knees feel weak with relief. Charlotte forgave me. I felt happy. I don't know if you have noticed this, but it is not always *easy* to be my friend.

"Charlotte, for real—how did you climb up that thing?"

It was diplomatic of me to return the conversation to her accomplishment. Plus, I really did want to know.

"I'm not even sure," Charlotte said. "It was like I slipped into this altered state of consciousness, and I was just going."

"Altered state of consciousness," I repeated. "No wonder Bonnie is interested in climbing."

"Well, I can see why," Charlotte said. "It was quite a feeling."

We walked quietly for a few moments.

"I guess I just better get over The Boy," I said.

"Why do you say that?" asked Charlotte.

"Because I've blown it twice now. There's nothing more I can do. There isn't any way to fix this."

"Don't be ridiculous," Charlotte said. "Want to know what your problem is?"

See, Dear Readers, this is a conundrum (a FABU-LOUS word that basically means a tough puzzle that doesn't necessarily have a concrete answer). If I say yes, Charlotte will actually commence to telling me what my problem is, and this can be, both conversationally and energetically, annoying. But if I say no, Charlotte will say nothing. She will not offer her thoughts on what my problem is. And between you and me, Dear Readers, I would actually like to know what my problem is. And Charlotte has a pretty good chance at knowing what it is. I made a decision.

"What is my problem, Charlotte?" I ask. Then I brace myself.

"Your problem is you think there is one specific Right Thing you have to do in order to get The Boy to like you. And that if you don't do this one specific Right Thing, or if you do it wrong, or if you try it and mess it up, then he'll decide once and for all that he does not like you and that will be it forever and ever."

"That's not my problem, Charlotte," I said. "That's my LIFE."

"No, Lily, it isn't," Charlotte said. "It's your INTER-PRETATION of your life. And it isn't accurate."

"Well then, what IS an accurate interpretation, Charlotte?" I asked, kind of huffily. I mean, I was supposed to be the advice columnist, after all. This was a little embarrassing. You know that thing they say—"Physician, heal thyself"? They don't say "Physician, Charlotte will now help you out."

"What is accurate is that you have to be Lily, at all times, and know that people who come into your sphere will see you for exactly what you are, which is a wonderfully talented, ambitious, and sometimes precocious artist who is occasionally a snappy dresser and who has a great deal to offer the world. The people who will want to be your friends, Lily, or even want to be your boyfriend, are the people who are the best matches for you. Not because they happened to see you carrying a copy of *Rock & Ice*, or because you said precisely the right thing at precisely the right time. But because they'll just know. Like I did."

Well. What does a girl say to that?

"Oh," I said.

I know there were other options, but "oh" was the shortest.

"Don't give up on The Boy," Charlotte added, unoffended by my monosyllabic response. "There's always another chance."

"I'm working at Ellis's again on Monday afternoon," I said hopefully. "I'll probably see him there."

"There you go!" said Charlotte.

"And at least we'll have something to talk about now," I added.

"That's right!" Charlotte said. "You now have a common interest. You're not just a distant *Rock & Ice* reader anymore—you were AT a climb!"

"I could ask him for some pointers," I said.

"He could be your coach!" Charlotte said.

I glowed. Charlotte was right. The way I saw things now, there was virtually no chance The Boy and I would NOT end up together. I looked around to confirm my feeling—yes, the world seemed a little brighter. The sidewalk in front of Charlotte's house shimmered.

"I should go in," Charlotte said.

We had a little hug, and Charlotte went.

I looked down at the sidewalk before starting home.

An ant was dragging another customer to the funeral home. Or maybe it was just one ant helping another one along. We all have bad days sometimes.

When I got home, my mother was sewing a tree skirt for a Christmas tree, even though it was mid-October. She was fresh from a Tree Skirt Sewing Seminar held in the basement of the local Episcopal church.

I know. I didn't know trees needed skirts either. I thought they were okay *au naturel*. But apparently it is considered quite untidy to put a Christmas tree in a stand and then allow the stand to be viewed in all its vulgar red-and-green metal shininess by friends and family. The proper thing to do is to put a little skirt around the tree stand, brightly decorated with the icon or holiday image of your choice, maybe a little glitter, and create the illusion that your Christmas tree is lithely springing out of a small mountain of homemade, hand-sewn felt.

How can I be biologically and genetically related to this woman?

"Here, honey," my mother was saying, pointing some kind of ray gun at me. "Wouldn't you like to put on a few pom-poms?"

"What is that thing?" I asked, taking a few steps backward. Maybe my mother hadn't been at a tree skirt sewing seminar after all. Maybe she had joined some space cult and had received a complimentary ray gun and was about to incinerate me, which in space language could be referred to as "putting on a few pom-poms." Should I run for it?

"It's a glue gun, silly," my mother said. "Come on. Have a pom-pom. I'm using white ones to decorate Santa's beard. I'm saving this big red one for Rudolph's nose."

The horror. THE HORROR!

But she is my mother, and she cares for me, and I did not want to destroy her pleasant craft-filled afternoon with a scathing, barbed comment. Besides which I didn't have one ready.

"No, thanks. I've got a book report I need to work on," I said.

My mother smiled happily and pointed the ray gun at Santa's head. I beat a hasty retreat, just in case. I didn't want to see Santa's felt image come to any kind of sorry end.

I went upstairs to my room and closed the door. In keeping with my new honesty policy, I had told the truth—I really did have a book report due. But I wasn't particularly worried about it. I had a LIFE to plan. Oh, and another Lily Pad letter to do, too.

I put on an Avril Lavigne CD—good music for being thoughtful and slightly brooding, but not in a counter-productive way. I lay on my bed with my hands clasped behind my head and made a mental list of things to do. First, I resolved to find a good book about the English Plantagenet kings and read it cover to cover. After all, how could I expect to be anything more than an errand girl for Ellis if I wasn't knowledgeable about the subject matter? Second, I planned to stop by the Astrology Hut today or tomorrow to buy some star and moon earrings. And maybe some sort of Peruvian-looking shawl, to create a nice layered look over the Mexican tunic.

And most importantly, I promised myself not to obsessively plan what I would say and how I would act the next time I saw The Boy. Charlotte was right. There was no One Right Thing I had to do for The Boy to suddenly like me. I just had to be me. Lily Blennerhassett.

Nice work if you can get it.

DEAR LILY,

I am getting terrible nightmares from reading Stephen King's books. I am worried that I am abnormal in some way. Almost every night I dream that I am in Maine and that something evil is chasing me. Last night I dreamed I was at an inn in Kennebunkport, and a clown with a monkey's tail kept trying to crush my head between two cymbals. Last week I dreamed I was trapped in a room with a girl with telekinetic powers who thought I had spread a rumor about her when really I hadn't, but she wouldn't believe me and she kept making her eyes turn red and stuff would fly around the room and hit me in the head. I fell asleep on the bus this morning, and I even had a little mini dream that there was a spider in my mouth.

What should I do?

NUTS OVER NIGHTMARES

DEAR NUTS,

Stop reading Stephen King!

Yours sincerely,

LILY M. BLENNERHASSETT

Eight

♡ LILY'S FANTASY INTERLUDE NUMBER THREE ♡

Lily is sitting demurely on the front steps of Ellis Parson's house. In the driveway The Boy is working on his bicycle, refitting the chain. Lily does not interrupt him, or bother him in any way. She loses herself in the quiet of the afternoon, embracing a deep inner peace.

But suddenly Lily's peace is interrupted by a feeling of foreboding. She scans the street anxiously but sees nothing. Concerned, she turns and looks at The Boy, who is kneeling on the pavement next to his bike. A dark movement catches her eye. Lily jumps up in horror. A long, lethal-looking rattlesnake is slithering toward The Boy's leg!

Lily calls out a sharp warning, but The Boy is wearing an Ipod and does not hear her. With no time to spare, Lily leaps

to her feet and rushes toward him, still shouting. Now The Boy does hear her, and he whirls around to face her, then follows her gaze to the deadly snake almost upon him, its rattle held high. The Boy tries to get up but loses his balance and tumbles backward. Lily rushes toward him, leaping between The Boy and the snake.

Lily feels only a burning prick above her ankle. The snake is slithering rapidly away. Lily feels strange, otherworldly. The Boy reaches over and lifts the cuff of Lily's jeans above her ankle.

Two fang-shaped wounds drip ruby liquid.

"Oh, my god!" cries The Boy. "You've been bitten!"

"I'm okay," Lily says weakly, but even as she speaks, she begins sinking to the ground. The Boy catches her, lays her gently on the driveway, and fumbles for his cell phone.

"Hang on," he says. "I'm calling 9-1-1."

"I'm fine," Lily says weakly, but she can barely speak above a whisper. She can feel the color draining from her face.

"Hurry," The Boy is shouting into the phone. "We need an ambulance NOW!"

The Boy takes Lily's hand between both his own. He squeezes, and Lily tries to squeeze back, but it is obvious she has very little strength left.

"You jumped between me and that rattler," said The Boy. "You stopped it from biting me."

"It was nothing," Lily murmurs.

"Who ARE you?" The Boy says with quiet urgency, cradling Lily's head tenderly.

"You know who I am. Your mother's assistant. Lily Blennerhassett."

"I know your name," The Boy said. "But I never realized who you were—who you REALLY were—until just now."

Lily's eyelids flutter.

"Stay with me," The Boy says. "I hear sirens—the ambulance is coming! STAY WITH ME, LILY!"

Lily tries to move her lips, but she can no longer speak.

"Lily, stay strong!" The Boy cries. "You're going to get better, do you hear? You're going to live through this! And when you're well again, maybe we can go get dinner and a movie!"

Even as she slips into unconsciousness, Lily manages a soft smile, which holds within it the answer "yes."

I got to Ellis Parson's house on time again on Monday, just in case. I wasn't all that surprised to find she wasn't home yet, but I was kind of surprised to find Bonnie sitting on Ellis's front steps. Was she there to see The Boy? My Boy?

"Hey, bud," Bonnie said.

"What's shakin', man?" I asked. I regretted the words as soon as they came out of my mouth. They sounded *ridiculous* coming from me.

"I mean, what's up?" I revised quickly. Bonnie didn't seem to notice my verbal editing.

"Jake asked me to stop by Colter's on my way home from school and pick up his biners and friends," she replied.

Beaners and friends? Was that some kind of vegetarian meal?

"Jake lent them to Colter," Bonnie continued, "but now he has a buddy who's going up to New Hampshire to climb, and he wants to lend them to him. Jake said to tell you hello, by the way."

Okay. I used my superior logical and deductive abilities to reason that beaners and friends were not a casserole but climbing equipment. Climbing equipment currently in possession of The Boy. Who could reasonably be arriving home any minute.

No obsessive planning of what to say and how to act, I reminded myself. I sighed, worn down with the weight of my undying passion.

"You still dig this dude?" Bonnie asked, moving a stray lock of hair from her eyes.

My mouth hung open for a minute. My first impulse, quite frankly, was to lie. But this was Bonnie, friend of past and present lives. I sat down on the step next to her.

"Yeah, I still dig him. He doesn't really seem to feel anything about me either way."

I was hoping Bonnie would protest here, telling me she'd seen him sneaking looks at me, or that Jake said the The Boy said—well, whatever. Said something. But

Bonnie didn't protest, she just looked at me and nodded.

"Just gotta turn it over, man. Either he's in your family or he's not."

"In my family?" I asked. Not always such a bragging point, wouldn't you agree, Dear Readers?

"Your family of consciousness. We all have one. I'm Sumari. There are dozens of different ones. Has to do with your spiritual makeup, you know, and what frequency you vibrate in."

"So if The Boy and I don't vibrate at the same frequency, we have no future together?" I asked.

"They don't have to be the same frequency. They just have to match. Like musical chords, you know. Going together. In harmony."

Harmony. But there could be no harmony if The Boy didn't show up, and right now I was vibrating solo.

"Is The Boy late?" I asked Bonnie.

"No idea, man. No watch."

Now this could mean either Bonnie carried no timepiece or she hadn't been looking all that carefully to see if The Boy was on his way. I opted to go with the former.

"You lost your watch?" I asked sympathetically.

"Nope, I don't believe in them."

"You don't believe in watches?" Who didn't believe in watches? I knew some people didn't believe in witches. But watches—I thought everyone believed in them. I didn't even know there was a choice.

"Actually, it's *time* I don't believe in," Bonnie clarified. "So watches are kind of pointless, know what I'm saying?"

I began to believe I would never know what Bonnie was saying. But there was always something about her that made me want to keep asking. Something that made me think if I ever *could* understand what she was saying, I might be making some kind of Huge Life Progress. Like Charlotte's rock climbing, but more abstract.

Maybe if I just waited and stared, Bonnie would continue. After a minute or so, when I thought she'd gone OOBE, my hunch paid off.

"You know, it's like all this physical stuff," she said, gesturing in the generalized direction of the world. "Like time, and space, and gravity, and the laws of physics, all that is just stuff we agreed to all believe in together to keep things organized while we're people, you know, while we're in the flesh."

"As opposed to . . ."

"Spirit," Bonnie said. "The way we were before all this, the way we'll be after. Here and now is just an illusion, man. Camouflage."

My mouth was going dry and my eyes were stuck staring at Bonnie's left earring. Have you ever gotten your eyes stuck staring at something—something you don't particularly *want* to be staring at, but you can't seem to make yourself look away?

I needed to speak to jolt myself out of the stare.

"Well, if there's really no time," I said, "and if we're spirit before this and after this, then we actually aren't really here now, because you just said there is no here and now."

I was actually being a tiny bit sarcastic, but Bonnie turned and looked at me with a gaze so rapturous, you'd have thought Joan of Arc had just materialized in the driveway. Bonnie actually clapped her hands together with joy.

"That's IT, man! You've totally GOT it! Look at you, dude, Lily Blennerhassett, describing the Nature of Reality! You blow me away!"

"Oh, yeah, well," I said, modestly. "You know. That's why they gave me the advice column to write."

Isn't that just my luck? I think I'm saying something sort of witty, and it turns out to be a description of the Nature of Reality.

"All right, there's my man," Bonnie said.

I thought she was still talking about me. But she was looking down the street, and when I did too, I could see The Boy riding his bike up the sidewalk. He didn't look like he had a vibrational frequency at all.

Pull yourself together, Lily. Pull yourself together.

"Am I late?" The Boy was calling as he biked up the

driveway. He got off the seat while the bike was still rolling and coasted up to the garage with just one foot on the pedal, the other leg slightly extended behind him.

"No idea," said Bonnie.

The Boy leaned his bike against the garage door and walked up the gravel path to us. He was wearing those crimson Converse sneakers again. This boy was magnificent. There ought to be little bluebirds flying in circles around his head, like in one of the old Disney cartoons.

Why? Why was this Boy magnificent when none other had been before him? Why had this particular Boy reduced me to grape jelly when we had barely exchanged one-syllable greetings? Why had I decided I couldn't live without this Boy when I didn't even know his vibrational frequency?

There was a bit of litter, a gum wrapper or something, just where The Boy was about to step. He reached down, picked it up, and tucked it into his pocket. My heart swelled with admiration.

"Got Jake's gear right inside," The Boy said to Bonnie, pulling a set of keys out of his windbreaker.

"Hi," I said, unintentionally loudly.

"Hey. Lily, right?" The Boy said, giving me a casual look. "My mother late again?"

HE REMEMBERED MY NAME. HE REMEM-BERED I WORK FOR HIS MOTHER.

Okay, not terrific accomplishments for a young healthy person who isn't suffering any severe short or midterm memory loss. He HAD brought me lemonade in his own house, after all. Not such a miracle he'd remember my name and who I worked for. Particularly when she was his mother.

But I had to seize on anything that was remotely positive. Speak, Lily.

"Yup," I said.

Smooth, no?

"Come inside to wait if you feel like it," The Boy said. "She could be forever, as usual."

He was asking me to go somewhere. Was that technically A Date?

We went inside. The Boy went upstairs to get the gear. Milo galloped down the hall, looking thrilled out of his beagle mind to see humans. He wagged his tail so enthusiastically, it kicked up a small breeze. He offered me his back to scratch while bending himself around to lick Bonnie's ankle.

"Dogs rock," said Bonnie.

"He throws up," I said. Bonnie nodded like she approved.

"Easy come, easy go," she said.

Hmm. That was one way I'd never looked at it.

The Boy came back down the stairs with a red duffel

bag slung over his shoulder. "It's all here," he told Bonnie, handing her the bag.

"Thanks, bro," she said. "Bet you wish you were going climbing in New Hampshire like Jake's friend, that lucky dog."

"You can say that again," said The Boy. "I haven't climbed Rumney in forever."

Bad. They were having a conversation in which I was not participating. This was bad, Dear Readers.

"Is Rumney sport or trad?"

Who said that? Who spoke?

The Boy looked surprised. Not half as surprised as I felt, though. Did I just say that out loud? Was I having a Brain Episode? Or was Milo indulging in a little beagle ventriloquism?

"Sport, mostly," The Boy said. "I thought you didn't climb."

"Haven't worked up the nerve to actually get myself on the rock yet. But I've read a lot about it. How scary can climbing actually be after writing an advice column, right?"

Who was operating my voice box?

But at least The Boy was looking at me.

"Advice column," he repeated.

Aha! A topic of conversation in which I COULD participate!

"I write a column called Notes from the Lily Pad, for the *Mulgrew Sentinel*," I said, making sure I kept my tone modest. But admit it, even with the modest tone, it must have sounded at least mildly impressive.

"Yeah. I don't really read that thing," The Boy said.

My mouth froze in a partially opened position.

"It's an excellent column. Lily understands the Nature of Reality," Bonnie said. Milo was staring up at her with his pool-like eyes. She was staring back at him. They appeared to be telepathically communicating.

I had been prepared to say all sorts of additional things to The Boy, but I had been momentarily waylaid by the news that he didn't read the *Sentinel*. Didn't *really* read, that is. What did *that* mean? Not often? Glancing without serious comprehension? Scanning? Mostly just looking at the pictures? What were we talking about here?

"I gotta motivate," said The Boy, glancing at his watch, "I'm supposed to be somewhere. Tell Jake I said thanks for the gear."

"I will," I said.

WHOOPS! How did that accidentally come out of my mouth when I knew perfectly well he was talking to Bonnie? What was WRONG with me?

Have you ever seen a TV show where a long, black car with tinted windows comes out of nowhere, and all four doors open and four big guys in dark suits and sunglasses get out and walk quickly and discreetly over to some person, surround him, and hustle him into the black car, which whisks him away to some secret government location?

I really, really needed that to happen to me right now.

"Bonnie will, I mean, won't you, Bon?" I asked.

Worse. WORSE. Made it worse by speaking again.

"Whatever," The Boy said. "Later."

Later. Right. Like, have a nice crossing on the *Titanic*, see you later.

"I'm going to get myself over to Sonia's farm, see what's sprouting," Bonnie said.

The Boy opened the front door and waited for Bonnie. I experienced a sudden moment of panic. All those possibilities Charlotte and I had discussed, and nothing had panned out, and The Boy was going! I felt like I was on one of those specials on Home Shopping Network, where I had to ACT NOW! TAKE CHARGE OF MY LIFE!

"So maybe you could give me some pointers on climbing sometime," I said to The Boy, who was still standing in the open doorway. "We could go back to the crag by the lake, and you could get me started?"

Yes! I had done it. How proud Charlotte would be, how RIGHT she was. And it was so easy—I just opened my mouth and asked. I was a GENIUS! I was a ROLE MODEL for all who were In Love!

The Boy shifted his weight from one foot to the other and looked over his shoulder outside, like he was expecting someone to be there. Then he glanced back at me.

"Yeah, sorry, I don't really have the time. Check the Yellow Pages—they might give lessons at the climbing gym. Later."

With that, The Boy walked out of the house. I was completely frozen in place, my mouth stuck half open in a stupid partial smile.

Bonnie brushed the top of my head with her slender fingers.

"Your aura's darkening, bro. Breathe, man. You need to unblock your chakras. The Universe is bending in your direction, and you need to remember that."

I nodded. Bonnie's words of comfort might just as well have been spoken in Urdu for all I could understand what they meant. But I understood her kind intention well enough.

Milo looked alarmed over these impending departures. I unfroze myself and knelt down next to him, draping an arm over his thick neck. He looked up at me and sighed happily, dosing me with a little blast of beagle breath.

"Later, bro," said Bonnie gently, following The Boy outside. The door closed, and they were gone.

Iceberg, dead ahead.

I remained kneeling next to the beagle.

"What just happened, Milo?" I asked. "How exactly did I do what I did? How did I go from conversational to rejectional in, like, under three minutes?"

Milo snuffled into the leg of my jeans and gave my knee a little lick. He sneezed and looked startled by the sound.

"Let's think through this logically," I said to him. He looked willing.

"Okay. The Boy came to the door and asked if I was waiting for Ellis. Then he asked if I wanted to wait inside. And I came in behind Bonnie. And up until then, Milo, we were *okay*. Don't you think we were okay at that point?"

Milo watched me with rapt attention, wagging just the very tippy top of his tail.

"Okay. Then The Boy went upstairs, and came down with the bag to give Bonnie, and said something about climbing. And I asked a question about climbing. Now jump in anytime if you disagree, Milo, but I think that we were still okay around then."

Milo did not elect to interject at this time.

"And then somehow I made the jump from climbing to writing an advice column. I think that's when the proverbial ocean liner came in sight of the iceberg."

Milo wagged his tail harder, and I am quite certain that by this he was indicating his agreement that I had correctly pinpointed the place where the conversation first became an enormous, doomed ship.

"And that's when he said he didn't really read the *Sentinel*. Which could have meant any number of things. Like he hadn't seen my column or didn't remember it, so he couldn't really say anything about it. Or, who knows, Milo, maybe he DID see it and didn't think much of it and was just too polite to say so. Maybe it was the Stephen King letter. That WAS a little flippant.

"And then I went out on a limb, Milo, and I asked The Boy if he'd teach me to climb. Essentially asked him out. And in case you happened to be scratching your ear during the next part, allow me to fill you in. He shot me down, completely. No 'maybes,' no 'we'll sees,' just flat out NO. Try the Yellow Pages. The Yellow Pages! I guess I better look under D, for DUH."

Milo leaned against my leg. He was beginning to look a little sleepy.

"It's just so EMBARASSING, Milo! So HUMILIAT-ING. What is it about me? I consistently REPEL the only person I'm trying to ATTRACT! The Boy has no problem socializing with Bonnie, right? He didn't seem to mind when Charlotte was the one who needed help with climbing, right? Okay, maybe she didn't need *that* much help. And maybe it was more Jake who helped her out. But still, every time I open my mouth around The Boy,

126

things seem to get worse. I've gone from Unnoticed to Undesirable. Why, Milo?"

Milo had not moved, but a distinctive smell was beginning to permeate the area.

"Ewww. Bad dog!"

Milo looked rather pleased with himself.

"Yick. All hands, abandon ship."

It was The Universe telling me to walk away from the subject. Or Milo's stomach was telling me it was encountering some difficulty in the digestive process. Either way, it was time to move on for the moment.

I stood up and went into Ellis's office, Milo plodding faithfully behind me. I noticed right away that there was a note taped to Ellis's computer monitor.

(Monday)

Hi, Lily,

If you're reading this and I'm not here, I'm sorry! I'm obviously running late again, and Colter has come by and let you in. But there are a few things you can do until I get back. There is a whole lot of crud stuck in my keyboard—can you dust it or just shake it upside down until it all comes out? There's also a new toner cartridge by the fax machine that I can't figure out how to load, and maybe you can. And if there's time *before I get back, I'd love one of those iced coffees from Starbucks. There's money in the jar by the printer.*

See you soon.

Ellis

P.S. There's a copy of my first chapter on the desk, if you want to read it.

Oh, man. This afternoon was getting worse by the minute. Now my job was sinking too. I should have read that Plantagenet kings book like I planned. Did Ellis not understand that I was dedicated, bookish, and articulate? Had I not assured her of my Impeccable Knowledge of Spelling and Grammar? And how was my Immense Bookish Talent being utilized? I was honing my Crud Removal Skills. Ellis didn't need me, she needed my mother!

I sat on the floor rubbing Milo's head and stewing in my own outrage. I could just leave, I thought. I could storm out. I could quit. Who would blame me? I was having a DEVASTATING day! And this was NOT what I had signed up for! I had enough on my plate already, with homework and the Lily Pad. And now this Vastly Disastrous Encounter with The Boy. If I had known being Ellis's assistant largely consisted of crumb control and coffee fetching, I never would have applied for the job in the first place. Who could possibly have a problem with me throwing in the towel?

Charlotte McGrath could, for starters. I could only imagine the lecture she would give me if I quit. I didn't want to hear more allegedly inspiring anecdotes from her experience interning at McCord, Chabon & List and her days at Young Executive Camp. In spite of myself, I could see Charlotte's lips moving earnestly in my imagination. She'd be throwing out words like commitment, perseverance, teamwork.

Then I thought of Bonnie, accidentally taking a nose-dive into the cow manure at Sonia's farm and considering it an inspiring work experience. Assuring me that The Universe was bending in my direction.

And what about The Boy? How would I look to him if I suddenly quit working for his mother? After all, I hadn't done anything to make him actively dislike me or hate me yet. He'd just told me, frankly and concisely, that he was unable to help me learn to rock climb. Okay. It was a bad sign, it was definitely not a GOOD sign, but it was not the end of the world. Maybe he thought I meant RIGHT AT THAT MOMENT. Maybe he thought I was suggesting we proceed IMMEDIATELY to the lake. He might have just misunderstood. I was simply in love with A Boy who had very little free time. And wasn't about to make any.

Then I thought of Ellis. In spite of the fact that she hadn't yet entrusted me with anything Extremely Important to do, she still seemed to think highly of me. She was the only Real Writer I knew. What would she think of me if I just bailed on her? I stared at the note she'd left and suddenly remembered something. In addition to crud removal, she'd asked me if I wanted to read her first chapter. Her just-written, as-of-yet-unpublished, real live first chapter! I WAS being given more responsibility! Could I possibly think of quitting now?

Milo was staring up at me with enormous Bambi eyes. He wagged his tail hopefully. His stomach made a little dog rumble, and he burped, licking his nose enthusiastically.

How could I leave All This?

With a sigh, I got to my feet, found chapter one, and stowed it in my backpack. Then I picked up Ellis's keyboard, turned it over, and began to shake.

Nine

I'd come up with various internal arguments as to why The Boy's not wanting to teach me to climb did not necessarily mean I had absolutely no chance with him. Unfortunately, the more I thought about it, the worse I felt. Charlotte called me the night it happened, and I crept into the Yakking Nook long enough to give her the basic details of the *Titanic* episode. I didn't really want to rehash the details, other than my offer and his rejection. Charlotte didn't seem to think things were as bad as all that. I knew it was possible she was right, but I knew it was also possible she was wrong, and I had been officially Rejected Forever. I was there. I was me. I was inside my head when it happened.

Day after day, I crawled from class to class like a sloth.

A very tired, bummed-out sloth. A sloth who used the tiny reserves of energy left in her to avoid The Boy successfully at school, to duck behind open lockers, dart into empty classrooms, and generally become invisible when he was in the vicinity. A sloth who was deeply relieved to be told that her after-school crumb-hunting services would not be required until the following week, as Ellis was flying out to a book conference. A sloth who did not even feel much excitement about reading Ellis's first chapter. A sloth to whom No Sane Person should write for advice.

When you think about it, the chances of being Lucky in Love are pretty slim. First, even though there may be this perfect-for-you guy floating around somewhere, he has to be in the SAME place that you are, at the SAME time. Not at the school three towns over, or doing a work study in Uzbekistan, but at YOUR school. Or at least in your town. (And forget living in the same century! You can really make yourself crazy figuring your One True Love was born in nineteenth-century France and lived out his life working as Napoleon's water boy). Then you have to actually MEET, which, depending on the size of your school, could be a miracle in and of itself. One grade difference in either direction could be disaster. Then, and here's a really tricky one, he's got to actually NOTICE you and consider you to be the perfect-for-him girl. Or at least to be interesting enough and cute enough to present that possibility. Then, of course, he has to be currently without girlfriend, currently without any complicated life situation which makes dating just too stressful and time-consuming and difficult, currently without any pressing extra romantic concerns whatsoever.

What are the chances of this happening?

Wait, don't tell me. I feel lousy enough already.

I know, Dear Readers. Things were bleak, but not hopeless, because I still had that Future World-Famous Author thing going for me. But in the Lily Blennerhassett Personal Life Arena, the forecast was dim, and I'll tell you why. Charlotte said I had to just be myself around The Boy, and I had. And you already know what happened.

Nothing.

If only I had worked up a scheme to be a little more Lindsay Lohan and a little less Lily Blennerhassett just for long enough to get The Boy's attention, and maybe score a date (or ten), and then once he was well and truly my boyfriend, I could gently and in small increments replace Lindsay Lohan with the real Lily Blennerhassett, which he would not actually notice except to feel that our relationship was deepening and becoming more poignant, mature, and spiritual, so that the end product would be The Boy plus Lily Blennerhassett equaling True Love of the Most Profound Nature, inspiring poems, songs, plays, and feature films. But I hadn't worked up that scheme. I had asked him to teach me to climb instead. And he had said no.

Which leads us right back to nothing.

So on Saturday morning I settled into my bed with a very fat feather pillow, a jumbo bag of peanut M&M's, and the first three Harry Potter books (yes, I read Astonishingly Fast, but I also wanted to plan for the option of not moving for many, many hours). I had opened the first book to one of my favorite scenes and popped a handful of M&M's into my mouth when my mother began calling from downstairs that Charlotte was on the phone.

Charlotte is my best friend, but I just wasn't ready for any more words of optimism and corporate wisdom. I wanted to soak like a Swedish meatball in my Gravy of Misery.

So I didn't answer.

I know you won't be surprised to hear that my mother kept calling me. She appeared suddenly, looming large in my doorway like the Loch Ness monster making an appearance at the surface of that Scottish lake.

"Lily, my goodness, didn't you hear me?" she said.

I gave her my most innocently startled expression, slamming the Harry Potter book closed with a shriek. The shriek may have been a little much.

"I've been calling and calling you," my mother said,

shaking her head. "Charlotte's on the phone."

"I can't really talk now," I said.

My mother looked at me like I'd spoken to her in fluent Serbo-Croatian.

"What?" My mother is one of those people who believe in taking phone calls, all phone calls, when you are home. You don't say you'll call back later. You don't have someone say you're not home. I needed some kind of excuse.

She would probably not believe that I was experiencing temporary paralysis, so I didn't try that one. I had one hand in a large M&M bag, so there was no use pretending I felt really, really sick. I'd already said something to her, darn it, so I couldn't claim to be losing my voice. I took a quick peek out the window. Maybe there was a tornado headed toward our house. An asteroid? An alien invasion? Something that would require our hasty evacuation?

Nothing in the air but clouds.

"Coming," I said. I knew when I was defeated. I would have to talk to Charlotte now, and she would know I had been stewing in my own misery, and she would have some plan ready to lure me out of the house and into some Meaningful Activity.

Well, they could make me talk to her, but they couldn't make me go.

"Hello?" I said.

"Lily? What took you so long? I've been waiting here forever!" Charlotte said, sounding outraged.

"Sorry," I said. "Moving a little slow."

"You've been sitting around stewing, haven't you?" said Charlotte.

Sometimes it is downright creepy the way she instantly knows stuff like that.

"I'm reading," I said.

"Reading what?" Charlotte asked.

I hesitated. Rereading anything for the third or higher time qualifies it as comfort reading. I knew it, and she knew it.

"Reading what?" Charlotte repeated.

"Harry Potter," I said quietly.

"Comfort reading!" Charlotte shouted. "You're coming out with me."

"I am not."

"You are, Lily Blennerhassett. Anyway, I have an offer you can't refuse."

"I doubt that."

"Shut up," Charlotte said. She can say that in a way that sounds very loving. "Bonnie called me, because she and her brother are going to that climbing place again and they thought I might want to go along. Which I do. And so do you."

"I do not," I said.

"The Boy is going," Charlotte said, playing her trump card.

"All the more reason for me NOT to go, Charlotte. The Boy does not like me, he does not have time for me, he does not place any import on my learning to climb, and he never will."

"You can't know that for sure if you stay holed up in your room," Charlotte said. "The only way to ensure nothing is going to happen to you is for you to DO nothing."

"Forget it, Charlotte," I said. "I'm over the pep talks. You go, and have a good time."

"I'm not going without you," Charlotte said. "And you ARE going."

"Charlotte, I'll say it one last time. THE BOY DOES NOT LIKE ME!!"

Charlotte gifted me with one of her deepest, most long-suffering sighs.

"Okay, Lily, maybe that's true. Maybe it isn't true. I certainly don't know. But okay. Let's say for the sake of argument that it's possible The Boy doesn't like you, in a boyfriend-girlfriend kind of a way. Does that mean you have to stay in your room from now on? Does that mean you have to blow off an invitation from your best friend? Like, since The Boy said he couldn't teach you to climb, everything is now pointless? Great chapter THAT will make in your memoirs."

"Actually, it would be a rather poignant and dramatic chapter, if handled tenderly."

"Let me put it to you in letter form. Dear Lily. I am a fourteen-year-old girl who thought she had met the boy of her dreams. Every fiber of my soul told me I was meant to be with this boy. Unfortunately, though I was brave and fabulous enough to ask him to do something with me, he turned me down. So my plan is to crawl into a cave, eating snack food and reading Harry Potter books for the rest of my natural life because I am now obviously without any real value in the world. What do you think? Sincerely, Moping Matilda."

"That's not a real letter," I said.

"Of COURSE it's not a real letter!" Charlotte shouted. "But how would you answer it?"

I hesitated, imagining I was at my desk at the Lily Pad, opening Moping Matilda's letter. Reading her sorry little words.

"Come on, Lily, be honest," Charlotte said. "Matilda's got a case of Twinkies and a year of *Teen People* magazines, and she's about to use them."

"This is stupid," I grumbled.

"Why?" Charlotte shouted. She didn't usually do this much shouting. I think the frequency and volume of her shouting increased after she started watching that Donald

Trump reality show—the one that always ends with him shouting, "You're fired!"

"Because it's too pathetic to be real."

"Put it in response form," Charlotte commanded.

"Charlotte . . ."

"In response form!" she barked.

Geez Louise.

I sighed. Sometimes you have to give the people what they want.

"Dear Moping Matilda," I began sourly. "Pull yourself together. No boy changes your level of importance in the world, and once you snap out of it, you will realize it is pathetic to think so. My meaning should be perspicuous even to someone at your level of emotional muck and mire. Come out of your cave and get on with your life. And get rid of those Twinkies. Do you have any idea the stuff they put in them to give them such a long shelf life? Sincerely, Lily Blennerhassett."

"What does perspicuous mean?" Charlotte asked.

"Clear," I said. "Not to be confused with perspicacious. A lot of people mix the two up."

"Well then, you are as perspicuous as the day," Charlotte said. "Aren't you?"

Okay, okay. Charlotte had cleverly used my own advice column (and my perspicacious abilities) to make her point. A shrewd, corporate-executive-level move. I knew when I was beaten.

"Fine. Potter and M&M's away," I said. "Where am I supposed to be?"

"We're meeting Bonnie on the library steps at two o'clock," Charlotte said, not bothering to disguise her triumph. "I knew you'd come to your senses."

"What choice did I have, when the Lily Pad answered the call?"

"Don't be late," Charlotte said quickly, hanging up without saying good-bye.

Well, there was nothing to do but get it over with. I changed into a clean pair of jeans and Jane Austen T-shirt and my Astrology Hut earrings.

It was unusually warm and humid outside for late October, and the damp had given my hair a mildly thrilling wave, so I didn't put it in a ponytail. Instead, I hung my head upside down and ruffled my hair at the roots, then flipped it back. The Astrology Hut sun and moon earrings shimmered subtly. Not bad.

So I had that going for me.

I hesitated in front of the mirror, sizing myself up, wondering what The Boy saw when he looked at me. Brown hair (wavy!), brown eyes (intelligent), a few freckles scattered across the nose, left over from summer sun. Not plump, but not tapewormishly thin. Everything looked more or less . . . Lily. Lily Blennerhassett. Take me or leave me.

"Mom! I'm going to meet Charlotte outside the library!" I shouted. Unnecessarily, it turned out, because my mother was coming *up* the stairs as I was starting *down* them. She had a ridiculously large feather duster in her hand.

"Have fun, be home by dinner, go inside if it thunders," my mother said all at once. The prospect of dusting obviously distracted her.

"Okay," I called, bounding down the stairs.

It did feel good to be moving again.

Watch or no watch, Bonnie and Charlotte were both already sitting on the library steps as I rode my bike up the sidewalk. I wheeled my bike over to the rack, locked it up, and joined them. Bonnie was eating sunflower seeds, and she offered me the bag. They looked too much like bird food, so I politely declined.

"I knew you'd come," Charlotte said. As if she had given me a choice. "Bonnie and I were just talking about dolphins. Bonnie went swimming with them."

"Today?" I asked.

I looked around, half expecting to see a few dolphins in sunglasses with towels slung over their backs walking down the street, waving their flippers at Bonnie as they went.

"In Mexico, man," Bonnie said. "Last winter break. There was this place you could go. And the dolphins

141 ❀

would swim all around you. Weaving in and out, poking their heads up right in front of you, making these clicking sounds. The energy coming off them was phenomenal! It was all intelligent and playful—really, really sharp. Like they totally understood why I was there, like they could feel my personality. I've never felt anything like it. Life ever really gets me down, man, I'm going back to Mexico to swim with the dolphins. Recalibrate my energy field. Total psychic makeover, man, in like thirty minutes. Changed the whole way I look at the world."

Charlotte looked entranced.

"Maybe you could start a business, Charlotte, transporting bummed-out people to Mexico to swim with the dolphins," I said.

"That is actually a very interesting idea," said Charlotte. "I could call it From Doldrums to Dolphins."

We all laughed. It was kind of a nice thought, swimming your troubles away with Flipper. I wouldn't mind having a crack at it.

The sky was rumbling. I looked up. It was getting positively dark, the clouds a stormy shade of green.

"Looks like a thunderstorm is coming," Charlotte said. "What's the safety protocol on climbing in approaching storms, Bonnie?"

It completely cracked me up to hear Charlotte using the words "safety protocol" in a question to Bonnie. They were so professional and efficient.

 142

"Protocol is No Way, José," said Bonnie firmly, examining the sky herself. "Jake had this buddy who was climbing out in Joshua Tree, getting a last route in before the rain hit, but there was all this electricity in the air, you know? So this guy is climbing up a crack in the rock face, and he plants a friend there—"

"A friend?" I interrupted. Half the mysterious duo of beaners and friends.

"Yeah, like this metal camming device you jam into a crack and it opens up and anchors itself in place, and you clip your rope to it as protection. So this bolt of lightning hits way at the top of the crag, travels all the way down the crack and into the friend, and *blam!* Blew Jake's buddy right off the rock, and he just hung there on the rope till his partner lowered him down."

"What happened to him?" Charlotte asked, wide-eyed.

"He was okay after a while," Bonnie said. "Melted the soles of his climbing shoes, though. Messed up his whole system. You wouldn't know it now to look at him, though, except his hair always grew in curly after that."

"No way!" I said. Bonnie looked at me with her pale, mystical eyes.

"It's true, dude. He had straight hair, and now it's curly. Lightning reset his hair follicles."

I was saved from further challenging this anecdote by the simultaneous appearance of several fat raindrops splattering by my feet and Jake and The Boy emerging from the path by the woods, bags of gear slung over their shoulders.

Have you ever heard anyone say "the sky suddenly opened"? I hate reusing standard descriptions, Dear Readers, but that is exactly what happened at that moment.

The sky suddenly opened, and in seconds we were halfway to drenched.

"Whoa!" yelled Charlotte, jumping to her feet.

Bonnie leaned her face back and extended her hands as the rain poured onto her face. She looked positively blissful. Jake and The Boy picked up their pace.

"I'm getting soaked," I yelled. I couldn't help it; my first thought was my hair. Those lovely waves. Flattened.

"It's only water, man," Bonnie yelled, her head still tilted, her face still ecstatic.

But suddenly it WASN'T only water.

There was this sizzling sound, like someone had tossed a giant slab of bacon into a football-field-sized frying pan. I felt stinging on my arms and neck, and I tried to slap it away.

"HAIL!" Charlotte cried. "It's hailing! Come on, inside!"

Jake and The Boy were now sprinting toward us. I jumped to my feet. Bonnie took a hailstone on the cheek.

"Ow," she said. "Dude, that hurt!"

I grabbed Bonnie and Charlotte by the arms, and we dashed up the stairs and through the library door.

Seconds later, Jake and The Boy burst through the door behind us. The five of us stood there dripping and rubbing the places the hailstones had hit us.

From the front desk, the librarian sternly regarded us over the top of her glasses. I didn't think she'd ask us to leave and drip elsewhere, but she didn't look particularly happy to see us. Kind of ungrateful, when you think there is a pretty good chance the place will one day be renamed the Lily M. Blennerhassett Library.

There was a table and some wooden chairs over by the periodicals section. I didn't think we could do much damage to them with our wet clothes.

"Come on," I said, leading the way.

They all followed me. Even The Boy followed me.

We settled in around the table. Charlotte sat at the head, like the dripping-wet CEO of a dripping-wet board of directors of a soaked corporation, about to commence its annual diving-board meeting.

"This sucks," said The Boy, smoothing his shining red hair away from his face.

"It's weather, bro," Bonnie said. "It's beautiful. Earth moods. From tranquillity to anger, nature style. Look out the window at that tree, dude! Look how the wind is bending it, look how the hailstones make each leaf tremble. Check out that lightning! Man, doesn't it make you feel totally alive and vulnerable? It's amazing!"

"It sucks," repeated The Boy. "What are we supposed to do now?"

"Plenty to read," said Jake, grinning at me as he slicked back his wet straw-colored hair.

"Reading sucks," said The Boy.

I actually felt my eyebrows shoot up to the top of my head.

"I knew I should have brought my homework, just in case," said Charlotte.

"Let's just rap, dudes," said Bonnie. "The Universe has organized this. We're supposed to be sitting here at this table together during a storm. There are no accidents, man."

Jake laughed.

"You think The Universe has gathered us together, eh, Bon?" he asked.

Bonnie nodded at her brother, and he laughed again. It was a nice laugh, though, a sweet laugh. Not a hah-hah-you-are-so-stupid laugh. It must be nice to have a brother like that, I thought. A brother who didn't think it was uncool to be your friend, even if you were somewhat unconventional. Like Bonnie.

"You don't actually believe all the stuff you come up with, do you?" The Boy asked Bonnie. He had propped his feet up onto the table, where the soles of his sneakers rained little drips of mud onto the polished surface.

I looked nervously at Bonnie, but she just glanced at

The Boy, her pale-blue eyes showing no irritation. She didn't answer him either way.

I decided to jump in.

"Well, hypothetically, Bonnie, what do you think The Universe might, you know, have in mind for us?"

Bonnie gave me one of her sleepy smiles.

"I don't know yet," she said. "That's the fun part."

"We need some kind of sign," I stated, grinning. The Boy was looking more and more bored, and we obviously needed some humor.

"O Universe," I intoned, spreading my arms wide and high, palms up to the sky. "O Universe that has gathered us here, give us a sign so that we may know your meaning. GIVE US A SIGN!"

All the lights went out.

Someone shrieked—one of those involuntary, high-pitched, there's-a-bug-in-my-sleeping-bag, absolutely GIRLY shrieks that pierce the air and the eardrum and cause everyone to jump practically out of their skins.

It was me.

"Lily, get a grip!" Charlotte cried. "It's only a power outage. You practically gave me a heart attack!"

I needed to finish hyperventilating before I could answer.

"I'm going to go talk to the librarian," Jake said, getting up. "Make sure it's okay for us to be here. Maybe she needs help with something."

While Jake was being a considerate and responsible human being, I waited for my heart to stop booming and my breathing to slow down. I felt like a racehorse running the Kentucky Derby.

It wasn't completely dark in the library by any means. There was a window by the table, and a skylight overhead. But the clouds were black outside, and even as my eyes adjusted, nothing inside looked very clear.

My mind was racing. I had asked for a sign, and clearly I had gotten one. But what did it mean? What was I supposed to be learning? That it was about The Boy I had no doubt, but what? Was I getting One Final Chance with him? Did I want a final chance? I rubbed my forehead, assuming as many highly intelligent people do that this might help me think more clearly. But Dear Readers, it did not.

"Lily," Charlotte said, noticing my rubbing. "Don't get freaked out. Power goes out in storms."

"But I had just asked for a sign," I said, still panting a little.

"It was just timing," Charlotte said.

I glanced over at The Boy, who was trying fruitlessly to find a signal on his cell phone. He snapped it shut, then opened it again.

Then I looked at Bonnie, who was watching me with interest.

"Bonnie?" I asked.

"There are no accidents," she said, smiling. "The Universe is speaking. It's cool, man. Enjoy the ride."

I knew it! Bonnie agreed. The Universe *was* speaking. But what was the message? I tried to analyze the sign logically. Okay. There had been a power failure. It was dark. It was difficult to see. I was looking around, but I wasn't seeing clearly. Was that my sign? WHAT DID IT MEAN?

Jake came back to the table.

"The librarian has a radio," he said. "The storm's been blowing through the county, with some pretty serious winds. She said we should all stay here. Shouldn't be too long before it's passed."

The Boy groaned. "Great," he said.

I don't think "great" was really what he meant. I think he was saying "great" while simultaneously thinking "this sucks," and he wanted us to know it.

"Let's go around the table and say what we want to be when we grow up," Charlotte said, smiling enthusiastically.

I felt a tinge of embarrassment for Charlotte as I glanced at The Boy to see how this suggestion was going over. He had slapped his hand over his eyes. Though I would never tell her this, Charlotte sometimes reminds me a tiny, tiny bit of my mother.

"You have to go first, then," said Jake. I thought it was

nice of him to go along with what was, let's be honest, a kind of dorky idea.

"I'm going to go to business school and get my MBA," Charlotte began. "Then I'm going to find work with an important corporation—not necessarily a huge one or an already established one or a famous one—just a corporation that's doing something and going somewhere. But after reading *The Economist*'s series on our current administration's sacrificing of our environmental concerns to the whims of big business, I've decided that whatever corporation I devote myself to must be environmentally friendly."

I had never heard that last part before. Wow. Charlotte was, in her own way, evolving.

"That's excellent," Bonnie said.

"Now you," said Charlotte, sounding pleased.

I could imagine any number of possibilities for Bonnie's career—psychic channeler, organic farmer, feng shui instructor, traveling yak milker.

"I'm going to be a doctor," Bonnie said.

The Boy laughed.

"Yeah, right," he said. I shot him a stern look he didn't notice, then looked at Bonnie. She seemed unperturbed.

"I'm going to be a doctor, man," Bonnie repeated. "Holistic. Mind, body, and spirit. Let people know there's more to healing than popping pills. Open them up to

 150

other things—herbs, acupuncture, reiki, meditation. That kind of doctor."

"Not a real doctor, you mean," said The Boy.

Geez Louise!

"I *do* mean," said Bonnie. "Four years of med school, get the degree, then become my own kind of doctor."

"Witch doctor," said The Boy. "I can't stand all that New Age mind-body crap."

Was there anything The Boy COULD stand? Other than rock climbing, which did not appear to serve humanity in any way?

"To each his own," Bonnie replied. "Lily?"

"As if we didn't know," said Charlotte. But she knew how much I loved to say it, and she let me.

"I'm going to be a writer," I said, grinning and basking in the fabulousness of it.

"Like the world needs another one of THOSE," said The Boy.

And.

That.

Was.

About.

ENOUGH.

All this time I had been working so hard to get The Boy to know Who I Really Was so that he would realize that he liked me. And I had probably failed. The Boy still

151

knew very little about me. But somehow, in the process, I had gotten a few glimpses into Who He Really Was. And what I saw, Dear Readers, DID NOT BODE WELL. I apologize to anyone I might upset by using strong language, but The Boy was kind of a butthead.

"Tell me something, Kilter, is it?" I began. The Boy looked at me with mild surprise.

"Colter," he said.

"What is it that makes you so cantankerous? So dismissive of everything? So thoroughly acrimonious?"

The Boy was now staring at me.

"I have no clue what you're yammering about," he said.

Translation: I do not know what the words cantankerous and acrimonious mean, and I have no intention of asking, or going home and privately looking them up in a dictionary at a later time, because I do not feel words are important.

Words ARE important.

"I'm yammering about you being mordant," I said.

He snickered, looked to Jake for support, and rolled his eyes.

And that, my friends, pushed me OVER THE TOP.

"Caustic," I said. "Derisive. Acidulous."

"Bilious," came Jake's voice. I shot him an astonished and, to be frank, slightly thrilled look. Bilious! Nice one!

"Vituperative," I said.

"Disparaging." Jake.

"Supercilious." Me.

"Excoriating." Jake.

"Malificent." Me.

"Contumelious." Jake.

I HAD NEVER HEARD THIS WORD BEFORE.

I stared at Jake in amazement. I had never met another walking thesaurus.

"Contumelious," I repeated carefully. Jake grinned.

"Excellent word, isn't it?" he asked. And he kept grinning.

The Universe chose this moment to restore electricity to the library.

The lights came on. The lights came on, and suddenly I understood the sign.

The Boy was not The Boy.

The Boy was NOT The Boy!

"This is lame," said Colter. "Power's back. I'm outa here."

"You should wait, bro," said Bonnie. "Storm still has some bite to it, man."

He got up anyway, pushed back his chair, looked at Jake.

"Spoken like a girl. You coming, Jake?" he asked.

I might have held my breath a little.

"Not into that mess," Jake said, nodding his head toward the window. "Besides, I'm not sure The Universe is done speaking to us, right, Bon?"

But he looked at me after he said it.

Colter shrugged and headed for the door.

"'Bye," said Jake. I don't think Colter answered.

"Later, Colder," I called. The door was closing behind him, so he probably hadn't heard.

"Jake's turn," Charlotte said.

"What?" I asked. "Turn for what?"

"To tell us what he's going to be," Charlotte said.

"Oh, it's spoiled now," Jake said. "We already have one at the table."

"You're going to be a doctor?" asked Charlotte.

"Nope," Jake said. "I want to be a writer."

He grinned at me again, but he put something sneaky into it because this time I could feel my face turning red.

"Yeah," he repeated. "I want to write."

I gave Charlotte and Bonnie a quick glance, then peeked at Jake.

And peeked again.

And that is when I finally got the whole picture. I understood what The Universe was trying to tell me when it turned the lights off and turned them on again.

The Boy was not The Boy.

Jake was.

Ten

Dear Readers, I, Lily Blennerhassett, was facing the moral dilemma of a lifetime. And shocking as it may seem, it had nothing to do with The Former Boy or The Real Boy. Nor had it emerged from my work dispensing advice from the Lily Pad. No, the moral dilemma of a lifetime turned out to be about Ellis.

Ellis hadn't needed me at all Thanksgiving week and had canceled a few other days too. The days I did go, sometimes I barely saw her at all, and just followed the instructions on her notes to unjam the fax machine or program the speed dial on the phone. Her lateness had become such a regular thing over the next month that she'd given me my own key to let myself in. In addition to making me feel important and trusted, this had the added benefit of not requiring The Former Boy to be around to let me in. Sometimes he showed up momentarily to get something, and he usually grunted a one-syllable greeting and was gone. Yeah. Like Bonnie said, easy come, easy go. Though she was talking about dog throw-up at the time.

Actually, Milo was turning out to be one of the best job perks. Each time I appeared, I was greeted with a level of exhilaration and joy I had never consistently inspired in any living creature. Milo practically fell over himself trying to wag his tail off, present his bottom to be scratched, and cover my neck with licks all at the same time. I had come to love everything about him, even his little flaws, which included having sudden, explosive sneezes that sprayed everywhere, and being very slightly pigeon-toed.

But Milo had nothing to do with the moral dilemma of the century. Like I said, it was Ellis. Or more specifically, Ellis's writing.

I had finally read the first chapter of her novel that she'd allowed me to take, and if my life hadn't been so completely distracting at the time, I would have paid more attention to how good it really was. But to tell you the truth, between The Former Boy and The Real Boy and the Lily Pad . . . I'd lost my focus a little. Kind of wandered off the path.

But Ellis had called and asked me to come at a special

time, and though I didn't usually work on Saturdays, especially with only three weeks of shopping left until Christmas, I'd agreed. She'd said she had something very important to talk to me about. But predictably, when I showed up at the agreed-on time, Ellis wasn't home. So I hung out in the office and chatted with Milo about how I felt very strongly that Jake was The Real Boy, as Milo listened with a confused furrow on his beagle brow.

When Milo got up and trotted out of the room, I didn't take it personally. I needed space sometimes too. So I started looking at all the books Ellis had on her bookshelf and was drawn to a journal of historical fiction that had a strikingly medieval cover. I pulled it down, sat on the floor, and flipped open to the table of contents. I noticed right away that there was an article marked with a pink Post-it note about Eleanor of Aquitaine by someone named Acton Bell. The name Acton Bell sounded familiar. Probably a well-known historian I had read. I turned to the page and began to skim it.

And then stopped in total disbelief.

The first paragraph of the article was almost word for word the same as the opening of the chapter Ellis had given me. I picked up the journal and read on. I found two more paragraphs that I'm sure were almost exactly reproduced in Ellis's book. This was no put-twenty-monkeys-in-front-of-twenty-typewriters-for-twenty-years-and-one-of-them-will-type-Shakespeare coincidence things. This was the gravest crime a writer could commit. This was plagiarism.

I'm ashamed to say, Dear Readers, that my first instinct was to call the police. Then, of course, I realized that stealing words generally does not get you handcuffed and tossed into the pokey. I thought of Trixie at Ellis's publisher. Should I call her? Did I have to say who I was? Could I send a note, or mail them the journal with a paper clip on the offending pages?

Could I, Lily Blennerhassett, make a citizen's arrest?

I needed to talk to Charlotte. In addition to always being able to make sense of a matter, Charlotte also had an unusually thorough understanding of the law, and she was the reigning master of ethics. I dialed Charlotte's number and impatiently waited while it rang.

Milo trotted back into the room and made his wide-eyed Disney face at me. I was sure he knew what I was doing. Preparing to hand his owner over to the literary authorities. And then what would become of him? How could anyone be capable of such cruelty to the world's most enchanting pigeon-toed beagle?

"Stop looking at me like that," I hissed as Charlotte's mom answered the phone.

She was so used to me being in the middle of conversations with myself that she didn't even ask me to repeat what I'd said. She just told me that Charlotte wasn't there, and that she'd been planning on dropping by Bonnie's house to borrow something before going to the library. So I called Bonnie's number.

"Hello?" Jake asked.

I had entirely forgotten that it is customary for brothers and sisters to live in the same house and to answer the phone when it rings.

"Hello?" Jake repeated.

"Phletamgah," I said.

Rats.

"Lily?" Jake asked.

Wow. I didn't know whether to be impressed that he knew it was me, Dear Readers, or totally mortified. Lily Blennerhassett, Phletamgah Girl.

"Hey," I said. It was the best I could do to recover. "I was actually looking for Charlotte . . . and her mom said—"

"Yeah, they just took off," Jake said.

"Oh," I said. "Okay. Never mind. I'll—'

"So how are you?" Jake asked.

What? Jake was asking me a question. Did I go for the standard "Fine," or did I tell him how, in fact, I was? I had to buy time.

"What?" I asked.

"How are you? What are you up to?"

"What am I up to?"

Why? Why? Why? I could talk to him normally before I realized he was The Real Boy, but now that I knew he was The Real Boy, I could no longer speak! Why?

"I'm at Ellis's," I said. "She's not here yet, and I just found out—I just needed to—I thought Charlotte . . ."

"Is something going on?" Jake asked. The guy had a kind voice. A kind and understanding voice. I could tell right away I needed to be careful when he asked questions, or before I knew it I'd be confessing to still sleeping with a stuffed monkey named Winky Bat, eating dry hot chocolate out of the canister with a spoon, and secretly worrying that my toes were not long enough.

"No," I said quickly. "I mean, you know. I don't know."

Then I just blurted it out. Jake appeared to take my discovery that Colter Hendricks's mother was stealing her new novel from the work of an old historical scholar in stride.

"Hmmmm," Jake said. "Let's think this through."

"I was thinking I could just mail the whole journal to her publisher," I said.

"I think you might be jumping the gun there a little," Jake said.

"Why?" I asked.

"Well, for starters, how about giving Ellis the benefit of the doubt for a minute? You're assuming the worst."

"What other explanation can there be?" I asked.

"I don't know," Jake said. "Maybe she has permission to use that article. You don't know."

"Maybe," I said. "But it doesn't seem very likely."

"There's something about that name, Acton Bell," Jake said.

"I've heard of him too," I said. "So he must be kind of famous. This could be a really big deal, Jake! I'm just going to mail the journal to the publisher and let them deal with it. Their address is right here. I'm just going to get it over with."

"You don't think you owe it to Ellis just to ask her first?"

"No," I said.

"No?" asked Jake.

I was starting to feel antsy, the way I get when someone wants me to do something the right way, but I am bound and determined to do it MY way.

"No!" I said. "I don't want to be involved."

"You *are* involved," said Jake.

"Ack! You're confusing me, Jake. Look, I'm just going to pack this thing up and mail it, and I need to do it now, because she could be home at any minute. I'll talk to you later thanks for the advice tell Bonnie I called and Charlotte if you see her 'bye."

And I hung up really fast.

Milo was still gazing mournfully at me.

"Cut it out!" I said. "This is a matter of honor, Milo, don't you understand that?"

Milo blinked sadly. He looked like the weight of the world was on his beagle back. I wanted to throw a blanket over his head so I wouldn't have to look at him looking at me, but there was no blanket handy. And time was of the essence. I opened Ellis's supply closet and grabbed a padded envelope. I was looking around for stamps when the phone began to ring. I ignored it. Where did Ellis keep her stamps?

After what seemed like forever, the phone stopped ringing. I found a pad of yellow Post-its on one of the shelves and opened the journal to the Acton Bell article. The phone started ringing again.

I tried to ignore it, but after about four rings, Milo went over to the phone and started barking at it. Have you ever heard a beagle bark? It is the loudest, most abrasive sound produced in the canine family. Fine crystal was probably shattering in Delaware. Even with my hands over my ears, the sound still hurt.

"All right!" I yelled at Milo, picking up the phone. Milo stopped barking instantly.

"Hello?" I said. "Ellis Parson's office."

"Why didn't you answer the phone?"

It was Jake.

"I did," I said.

"Not a minute ago," Jake said.

"Jake, Ellis could be here any second, so—"

"Yeah, it's about that. Listen, Lily, I really think you need to talk to Ellis before you do anything."

Why today of all days did I have to learn that Jake was a do-the-right-thing kind of guy?

"Jake—"

"You owe it to her! Think about it, Lily, what if you're wrong? And you send that journal off to the publisher, and you never even asked her about it? And you went and accused her of plagiarism falsely and she finds out about it from them? Is that the way you'd want someone to treat you? Is that what you want to be known for?"

Was Jake right? Did I owe Ellis more than this? Wait a minute—was I assuming that because The Boy was NOT The Boy, that Ellis was NOT a Real Writer?

Beam me up, Scotty, beam me up.

"And another thing," Jake said. "I remember now why that name sounds familiar, Acton Bell."

"Because he's a noted historian?" I asked.

"No. Because Acton Bell was the pseudonym of Anne Brontë. Remember?"

Believe it or not, I actually did remember.

"That's right," I said excitedly. "All three Brontës wrote under pen names . . . Acton Bell, Currier Bell, and . . ."

"Ellis," said Jake. "Ellis Bell."

Ellis.

"Okay, wait . . ." I said. "What does that mean?"

"I have absolutely no idea," said Jake unhelpfully. "But you know what Bonnie would say?"

"That it's The Universe trying to get my attention," I said. "Trying to get me to think."

Jake laughed. Oh, nice, nice laugh. I suddenly realized I'd been so caught up in my dilemma, I'd forgotten Jake was The Real Boy, and I had therefore actually been having a conversation with him. Phletamgah.

"Exactly. And if The Universe is trying to get your attention, maybe you better hold off on mailing that package."

I heard the front door open, and Milo dashed out of the room like a shot.

"Oh, man, I think she's home!" I whispered.

"Lily, just ask her, okay? Promise me you'll ask her."

I heard footsteps coming down the hallway, and I put the phone down without saying good-bye.

"Darling!" Ellis said. "Are you going to kill me? Late *again*!"

And then she hugged me, smelling of wildflower perfume and laundry detergent. Her long crystal-and-silver drop earrings swayed gently as she smiled at me. She had a tea-colored, hand-crocheted shawl draped over her shoulders. Her reading glasses hung from a glass bead chain around her neck. She was fabulous. Simply fabulous.

"I am so sorry," she said. "Everything is even crazier than usual. And you give up a Saturday morning for me, and I can't even be here on time for *that*!"

"It's okay," I said, looking down.

I felt so embarrassed. Honestly, I didn't think I could feel any worse than I had with Milo giving me the Disney stare while I prepared to betray his owner. But now that Ellis herself was here, beaming and apologizing, I felt lower than ever. How could *she*? How could *I*?

"You're going to kill me," said Ellis, and I looked up at her in surprise.

"Why?" I asked.

"I got the call last night. I've been awarded a writer's residency at a university in England," she said. "Eight months of light teaching, all expenses paid plus modest salary, with my own apartment, and access to the university's medieval archives. Starting just after Christmas break! I'm barely covering the rent here as it is, and I won't even get paid my second advance until I finish this manuscript. Now I've got money, a place to live, and research being handed to me on a platter."

But that sounded like great news. Ellis had to be not only a Real Writer, but a Real Writer of Immense Talent to be offered a deal like that.

"It all sounds perfect. So why am I going to kill you?" I asked.

"Well, honey, it's the opportunity of a lifetime, and I've got to take it. But I obviously can't bring you along," she said. "Which makes you about to be out of a job, and I know it hasn't been a very good job so far. All that experience I said you were going to get. When so far I only got around to sending you for coffee. I thought we'd get to all that, you know. I didn't know there wouldn't be any time."

Me. She was thinking of me! I loved this woman.

"It's okay," I said. "I still have my job at the school paper,"

Ellis sat down and sighed.

"I know, Lily. But it would have been nice. For me, I mean. For me, too. I was looking forward to working with you. You remind me of myself when I was young and so sure I wanted to be a writer, everything still in the future. We would have made a good team, if I'd been better organized. I've really let you down."

I really wanted Ellis to stop being nice to me. Because I knew what I had to ask her. Milo, for the time being, had fallen asleep—a small blessing. I don't think I could have handled the guilt of seeing both of them simultaneously.

"I never even asked you if you got a chance to read my chapter," Ellis said.

I froze. Thought of Jake telling me to just ask her.

"I did, actually," I said. "I really liked it."

"Did you?" Ellis asked eagerly. "Really?"

"I did," I said. "There was—I mean, I did wonder about—"

"What?" Ellis asked. "You can ask me anything, Lily. Writer to writer. I won't be offended."

Writer to writer. Why not just kick me in the stomach and get it over with?

"Well, it actually has to do with—Acton Bell," I said, watching her face closely.

"Acton Bell?" Ellis asked.

I heard Jake's voice again in my head, advising me to just come out and ask. I picked up the old journal and opened it to the page with the pink Post-it.

"You read my article?" Ellis asked.

"Your article? It says it's written by Acton Bell," I said.

Ellis laughed. "My first pseudonym," she said. "My pen name. It was Anne Brontë's pen name, actually. Her sister Emily Brontë wrote under the name Ellis Bell, and the third sister, Charlotte, wrote under the name Currier Bell. I love the Brontës, so that's why I picked one of their pen names. I couldn't be Ellis, of course; that was already me. I wrote this article fifteen years ago on spec—got twenty-five dollars for it. I was so worried at the time that it would get panned, I was afraid to put my name on it.

The journal, of course, sold about seventy-five copies, and until today I've never met a living soul who's even read the article. Which is fine with me—it really is kind of a pretentious piece; I was so young and so arrogant when I wrote it! But even so, there are some great bits here and there. I lifted some of them for my opening chapter."

She'd stolen them from herself. Jake and The Universe had probably just saved me from doing a hideously embarrassing and just plain flat out BAD thing because I hadn't trusted Ellis enough by myself. I had written her off, along with her butthead son.

Dear Readers, I felt smaller than plant food.

Ellis was still talking.

"And on top of that I have to get all this packed up, find someone to handle the house rental . . . what a mess. Colter is going to have to move back in with his dad again in New Paltz, which, to be honest, he's wanted to do from the start. He never wanted to leave New Paltz in the first place, and frankly he's been surly and unpleasant to be around ever since we moved here."

It had never occurred to me that The Boy might have a REASON to be a butthead. I suddenly felt a tiny bit defensive on his behalf.

"Oh, he's not so bad, Ellis," I said. "You know what I've noticed about him? When he sees a bit of litter on the ground, he always picks it up and gets it to a trash can."

The smile Ellis gave me was like a sunrise.

"He does do that, doesn't he?" she said. "I'd forgotten. He's got a good heart underneath. I can't blame him for being impatient with me. It's not easy having a writer for a mother, Lily, I can guarantee you that."

I wanted to say that I couldn't imagine anything more fabulous than having a Real Writer for a mother. But it also wasn't the worst thing in the world to live in a very tidy house where clean clothes are always plentiful and all the food groups are served with every meal and on time meant on time.

"And then there's the problem of Milo," Ellis continued, rubbing the top of her head and looking fretful.

"What about Milo?" I said, snapping suddenly to attention.

"I can't take him overseas," she said. "And I hate to have him go with Colter's father. I mean, he'll be taken care of, but I don't think he'll really be loved, you know? Beagles live for affection. And I certainly can't just take him to the pound. What am I going to do?"

My heart was thumping. I knew the responsible thing to do was to talk to my parents first. I knew it wasn't right just to jump into that kind of commitment without checking with anybody. But I couldn't hold myself back.

"I'll take him. I'll take him!" I shouted. "Can I take him, Ellis? Please?"

Ellis looked astonished, then thrilled.

"Is that going to be okay?" she asked.

"Milo LOVES me," I said. "It will be fine!"

"Oh, Lily!" Ellis cried. "I'll be so happy knowing he's with you. Do you want to go and live with Lily, Milo? Do you want to go live with Lily?"

Milo looked back and forth between the two of us, bright eyed, his tail wagging frenetically. He stifled a burp.

I knew that this was all part of The Universe's plan.

Now I just had to explain it to my parents.

Eleven

Lily and The Real Boy are sitting in a bookstore. At a long table in front of them are piles of books. They are all copies of the same title. A long line snakes through the bookstore and out onto the sidewalk; people are waiting to get their books autographed by the famous coauthors. A little old lady takes the book Lily has just signed and thanks her repeatedly. Lily looks up at the next person in line and gives a little feminine gasp of surprise.

"Ellis!" Lily cries. "I can't believe you made it!"

"Would I miss this?" Ellis asks, making a delighted gesture around the bookstore. "New York Times bestseller list, National Book Award finalist, Sofia Coppola already offering for film rights? Lily, I'm just so proud of you!"

"Well," Lily says modestly, "I did have some help." Lily and Ellis beam at Jake, who glances up from the book he is signing and flashes them a heart-stopping grin.

"I don't want to hold you up," Ellis says. "There are so many people waiting to get books signed."

"Oh, but come to the party afterward!" Lily cries. "It's at The Gotham."

"Lily, you are indeed a wonder," Ellis says. "I will see you both at The Gotham."

As Ellis steps away from the table, the next person comes into view.

It is The Former Boy.

"Name, please?" Lily asks, opening the book to sign.

"It's me," says The Former Boy.

Lily looks up.

"Is that spelled the way it sounds, or is it M-E-Y?" Lily asks.

"No, Lily, it's me," The Former Boy says. "Don't tell me you don't remember."

Lily looks up and studies his face.

"Ah, yes," she says, picking up her pen again. "Is that Canter with a C?"

"Colter," The Former Boy says.

"'To Coultter,'" Lily reads as she writes. "'Best wishes, Lily M. Blennerhassett.'" She hands him the book. "Enjoy."

The Former Boy doesn't move.

"Did you need something else signed?" Lily asks in her

special patient voice. She discreetly looks around The Former Boy to see how many people are still waiting.

"No," The Former Boy says. "I just . . . I can't believe you wrote this."

"Jake and I wrote it together," Lily corrects, still peering around The Former Boy.

"Yeah, I know. I mean, I've been reading about this book everywhere. It's like, huge! I heard Sofia Coppola wants the film rights."

Lily makes her tight, no-longer-so-patient smile and taps her pen firmly on the table.

Tap. Tap. Tap.

"Listen, I won't take up much of your time," he continues. "I can see there's a ton of people waiting here to see you. I just wanted to ask, Lily, if maybe you'd be interested in going to dinner and a movie sometime?"

Lily stops tapping her pen and looks up at The Former Boy. She smiles her most tender smile.

"That's sweet, Candor. But no. No, thank you. The answer's no."

"No?" The Former Boy repeats, as if he doesn't believe it. "Why?"

"Why, Colder, there's a veritable plethora of reasons, if you're familiar with the word 'plethora,' as it's a very good one. But let's just stick with the simplest reason."

Lily reaches out and takes Jake's hand.

"My boyfriend wouldn't like it."

"Oh, so that's how it is," The Former Boy says angrily.

Jake stands up and rises to his full six-foot height. He stares at The Former Boy in silence.

"That is how it is," Lily replies.

"Whatever, man," The Former Boy says. He tosses his signed copy back onto the pile. "You can keep your stupid book. I wasn't going to read it anyway, I was just going to sell it on eBay."

The Former Boy strides off angrily, and Lily and Jake exchange a look of understanding, compassion, and a modicum of sadness.

"I understand," says The Former Boy sadly. "I guess I always knew. But I had to try, Lily. I had to try."

The Former Boy looks at the signed book he is still holding in his hands.

"I'm going to take this home and read every word," he says. "Every one. I don't care how long it takes me. I've never been a reader, I've never thought books were anything but crap. But you wrote this book, Lily, and that means something to me. I'm going to read it."

"Oh, Calvin, that's wonderful," Lily says. "I do hope you like it. You can post a review on my website if you like."

"I'll do that," says The Former Boy. "Thank you, Lily. For

everything, I mean. Thank you."

Lily smiles and nods, and The Former Boy walks slowly away.

Lily and Jake exchange a look of understanding, compassion, and a modicum of sadness.

"A beagle?" asked my father.

"A beagle?" repeated my mother.

I had done my research, and I was ready to present it. My father was allergic only to cat hair and studies showed most dog allergies resulted from sensitivity to dog dander, and that many people allergic to cats had no problems living with dogs. I had a printout and a nice graph Charlotte had made for me in my pocket.

From an Internet source, I had learned that beagles are one of the cleanest breeds of dogs. They are fastidious about grooming themselves and are also fond of licking anything they come in contact with, making them nothing less than a live-in furniture and floor polisher. Those facts, along with the photograph I'd downloaded of a beagle licking crumbs from a hard-to-reach kitchen corner, ought to give my mother cause for consideration.

They were small, but not lapdog small. They were loyal. They were friendly. They were smart. They were good watchdogs. They were trustworthy around small children. They could exercise themselves in a properly fenced-in yard. And Milo himself was along in doggie form to attest to the diabolical cuteness of his breed.

I had all these facts ready to fire rapidly at both my parents, but when I faced them to begin my verbal assault, I found them both on their knees, one on either side of Milo.

My mother was speaking in what can only be described as high-pitched, grammatically devastated baby talk.

"He's a widdle chicken! He's just a widdle chicken!" she cooed, rubbing her face on the top of Milo's head.

Geez Louise. Not only was she speaking badly in baby talk, she was also misidentifying the animal family to which Milo belonged.

My father, on the other hand, was talking in a gruff, masculine tone you might expect from a Little League coach trying to show his players affection without losing their respect.

"Good buddy, arencha? Good bud, yep. Good little man, yessiroonee," he intoned.

"The handsomest chicken on the farm!" my mother squealed, squeezing Milo's velvet-soft ears.

Really, I didn't know whether to feel happy they seemed to like the dog, or to be utterly terrified at their bizarre and extremely unappealing personality changes.

"I'll take care of him," I said, realizing I sounded just

like the kid in the book *Shiloh*, which Dear Readers may note is also about a beagle who needs a home. "I'll feed him, brush him, vacuum up all his dog hairs, and I'll walk him three times a day."

"Oh, I don't think so," my mother said, lifting her face about a half inch off the top of Milo's head to look at me.

It was the vacuuming thing. The dog hair. I knew that was going to be my biggest obstacle.

"Mom . . ." I began.

"Lily, if this dog is going to be living here, you don't get to hog him all to yourself," my mother said. "I want to walk him too, you know. And brush him. And fill his bowl with kibble and watch him eat wif dose widdle doggy lips."

Ew.

"I want to walk him too," said my father. "Great way to get exercise and companionship at the same time."

I could hardly believe what I was hearing.

"Wait," I said. "Are you saying . . . does this mean we can keep him?"

"We're keeping him," my mother cried. She rained kisses onto Milo's nose. "Christmas is only three weeks away, and what a present! We couldn't turn away such a widdle chicken!"

I jumped up and clapped my hands with delight.

"Milo! You're staying!" I shouted.

Glee is infectious, and Milo instantly jumped up too, and began trotting toward me. He slowed after a few steps, and hiccuped. He stood with his legs slightly splayed, his head lurched forward a little, and his stomach quivered.

"Wait just a—" started my father.

"Is something—" my mother began.

Milo dropped his head, took one little stagger, and threw up a grass ball onto the floor. Then he keeled over and lay motionless on his back, all four legs in the air.

I turned to my parents, who were staring at me with abject horror.

"I can explain."

A few weeks later, the last issue of the *Mulgrew Sentinel* before Christmas break was coming out. Charlotte, Bonnie, and Jake gathered around my Lily Pad desk to celebrate. We had plastic glasses of diet Vanilla Coke (a horrible vending machine misunderstanding) with which to toast.

"To wisdom from an old soul," said Bonnie, and we clinked and drank.

"To the business of self-improvement," said Charlotte, and we clinked and drank.

"To the written word," said Jake, and we clinked and drank.

 178

"To my Dear Friends and Readers," I said grandly. Clinked. Drank.

Yeah, I know. It would have been nice to have some kind of toast in there to Love. Maybe Jake saying "To Lily." Or Lily saying "To Jake." Or "To my boyfriend." Yeah, that might have been nice. But it hadn't happened.

Then again, it hadn't NOT happened. You might say Jake and I were still an open book. We talked on the phone together, ate lunch together, yakked about books together. He had even offered to give me a climbing lesson, but I said I wanted to wait until the weather got warmer. It took time to figure out exactly who a person was. The more I found out about Jake, the more convinced I was that he was, in fact, The Real Boy. And every once in a while I'd catch him looking at me in a way that made me wonder if he was thinking I might be The Real Girl.

But The Universe is taking its time on this one, and I have to say, Dear Readers, I'm kind of enjoying it. I still believe in love at first sight, but I've decided to remove myself from the eligibility list. All those cupids slinging all those love arrows at huge groups of people who look more or less alike. It's no wonder there are the occasional cases of mistaken identity.

"So what's your last column, dude?" asked Bonnie.

"You didn't get any more of those paste-eater letters, did you?" Charlotte asked.

"Nope. Paste-Eating Pastime has either been cured through the pearls of wisdom delivered him or her via the Lily Pad or has glued all his or her fingers together and is no longer able to communicate. My last column, actually, is a letter from me."

I paused for dramatic effect.

"Lily Blennerhassett."

Can't help it, Dear Readers. I've always liked saying my name. It makes the ends of my toes warm.

"Well, let's see it," said Jake. "Don't be shy. Hand it over."

"Alas, I can extend no special privileges even to my most devoted readers," I said. "You'll just have to wait until the paper is distributed."

"Unless we intercept the distribution vehicle, which happens to be parked yonder by the Coke machine," said Charlotte. She jumped up and made a beeline for the wheeled cart holding the new edition of the *Sentinel*, hot off the press.

"Me too!" said Bonnie, jumping up and running to the cart.

"Boys first!" called Jake, taking off after Bonnie.

That left me sitting alone at the Lily Pad. I smiled as I watched them pull papers off the cart and fight over them.

This was a good moment. A writer's moment. I sat

alone at my desk, with my work. But soon I'd be surrounded by friends.

DEAR READERS,

Merry Christmas from the Lily Pad. You've sent me so many carefully crafted letters, so I thought it was time I wrote you one.

First semester is just about over, and I can't think of a time I've learned more. Since I'm in a position of authority and published in a widely read periodical, I'm going to take advantage of my power and tell you a few key items of wisdom I've recently acquired.

1. The Universe is always trying to tell you something important. Make sure you are not wearing your Ipod when the message comes through.

2. If you are going to judge a book by its cover, make sure you follow this up by reading the book IN ITS ENTIRETY before finalizing your judgment.

3. If someone you respect and admire appears to have done something wrong, do him or her the courtesy of speaking to him or her about it directly before freaking out and doing something

ape-wad that may well get you into an embarrassing if not downright slanderous situation
after the fact.

4. Remember that no one is ALL good or ALL bad.
   Even a total butthead sometimes picks up litter.

5. When a good friend urges you to get out of bed
   and stop marinating in your own misery, follow
   her instructions to the letter, then buy her a
   nice gift.

6. If you see a beagle lying on its back with all four
   paws in the air, do not assume it is dead. If it is
   my beagle, Milo, it has only fainted.

7. Do not rock climb during a thunderstorm.

8. Never give up on love.

                        Season's greetings,
                        LILY M. BLENNERHASSETT

THE LILY LIST:
Words to Live By
(in order of appearance, as defined by
*Merriam-Webster's Collegiate Dictionary, 11th Edition**)

infantilize: . . . to treat as if infantile (**infantile:** of or relating to infants . . .)

malaise: an indefinite feeling of debility or lack of health often indicative of or accompanying the onset of an illness . . .

persnickety: fussy about small details : FASTIDIOUS . . .

contemporaneously: existing, occurring, or originating during the same time

quixotic: foolishly impractical esp. in the pursuit of ideals; *esp:* marked by rash lofty romantic ideas or extravagantly chivalrous action . . .

termagant: . . . an overbearing or nagging woman : SHREW

perspicacious: of acute mental vision or discernment : KEEN

Brobdingnagian: marked by tremendous size

hyperbole: extravagant exaggeration

resplendent: shining brilliantly . . .

opprobrious: deserving of opprobrium (**opprobrium**: something that brings disgrace . . .) : INFAMOUS

conundrum: . . . a question or problem having only a conjectural answer . . .

perspicuous: plain to the understanding esp. because of clarity and precision of presentation

* By permission. From *Merriam-Webster's Collegiate® Dictionary, Eleventh Edition* © 2004 by Merriam-Webster, Incorporated (www.Merriam-Webster.com).

cantankerous: difficult or irritating to deal with

acrimonious: caustic, biting, or rancorous esp. in feeling, language, or manner

mordant: biting and caustic in thought, manner, or style : INCISIVE . . .

caustic: . . . marked by incisive sarcasm . . .

derisive: expressing or causing derision (**derision:** the use of ridicule or scorn to show contempt . . .)

acidulous: somewhat acid or harsh in taste or manner

bilious: . . . of or indicative of a peevish ill-natured disposition . . .

vituperative: uttering or given to censure : containing or characterized by verbal abuse

disparage: . . . to depreciate by indirect means (as invidious comparison) : speak slightingly about

supercilious: coolly and patronizingly haughty

excoriate: . . . to censure scathingly

maleficent: working or productive of harm or evil : BALEFUL

contumelious: insolently abusive and humiliating

plethora: . . . excess, superfluity; *also*: PROFUSION, ABUNDANCE

Words Not Currently Listed by Merriam-Webster

phletamgah: a nonsensical exclamation often associated with confusion brought on by finding oneself on the Brink of Love